# AWAITING DEVELOPMENTS

Judy Allen has worked in the theatre, in publishing and in a literary agency. But for several years she has been a full-time writer, and now has over twenty books – some fiction, some non-fiction – to her name.

As you might expect from a writer of guidebooks, place plays a very important part in Judy Allen's stories: "More often than not, the setting becomes one of the main characters," she says. This is certainly true of *Awaiting Developments*, in which the main character, Jo, fights to save a beautiful garden from urban property developers. The book's strong ecological theme won it the Friends of the Earth Earthworm Award and it also won a prestigious Whitbread Award.

A full-time writer, Judy Allen lives in Putney.

Also by Judy Allen

*The Dream Thing*
*The Lord of the Dance*
*Something Rare and Special*
*Song for Solo and Persistent Chorus*
*The Spring on the Mountain*
*The Stones of the Moon*
*Travelling Hopefully*

Books for adults

*December Flower*
*Bag and Baggage*

# AWAITING DEVELOPMENTS

## JUDY ALLEN

**WALKER BOOKS**
LONDON

First published 1988 by
Julia MacRae Books
This edition published 1989 by Walker Books Ltd
87 Vauxhall Walk, London SE11 5HJ

© 1988 Judy Allen
Cover and inside illustration by Sharon Scotland

Printed in Great Britain by
Cox and Wyman Ltd, Reading

British Library Cataloguing in Publication Data
Allen, Judy
Awaiting developments.
I. Title
823'.914[F]
ISBN 0-7445-1321-9

# CONTENTS

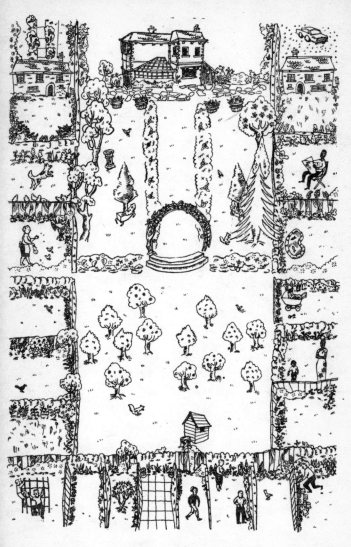

*The Big House (top)*
*showing the garden and surrounding houses*

# CHAPTER ONE

It isn't easy to get any privacy in a house like ours. It's too small and there are too many people in it. But about three years ago I developed this special technique which worked very well, I thought, though it was a bit of an effort, and not something I liked to do very often. For one thing it really needed good weather, and for another, it seemed to me that the more I did it, the more likely I was to be found out. I can remember the last time I did it properly.

It was Easter Saturday. Mum was making a tremendous performance of shampooing the carpet in the middle room. Dad kept appearing in the doorway of the front room to say that the telephone didn't seem to be working. Sam was entertaining a friend everywhere else in the house. They were all beginning to get on my nerves.

Me, I was sitting trying to read at the table in the kitchen, which is at the back of the house. The wall which had originally divided the kitchen from the middle room had been partly bashed away, years ago, to leave a big square arch, so nobody in either room is really separate from anybody in the other. Apart from the fact that we always eat in the kitchen, and that the sofa and TV are in the middle room, the two rooms are really one.

I'd chosen the kitchen end because in the daytime the kitchen is lightest. It has a long window, above the sink, which looks out over what we call the garden. It has grass, and a hydrangea bush, and a fence all round, so there really isn't anything else you can call it – but it's so small that when Sam sneezed once out of the open kitchen window, the spit hit the end fence. Of course that may say more about Sam than about the garden.

The middle room window looks out on to a short passage between the outside wall of the kitchen and next door's fence. Every year Mum fixes pots of geraniums into metal loops she's stuck into this fence, and quite often they don't die till as late as July. No sun, a permanent draught, and dark brown creosote are very discouraging to geraniums, it seems.

The lightest and best room of all, of course, and the one everyone else in the terrace uses as a living room, is the front room – but that's Dad's office and it can be out of bounds if he's busy.

What with all the froth and vigour in the middle room, all the moaning about the phone from the front, and Sam and what's-'is-name everywhere else, it was clearly time to get out.

I banged on the table with the spine of my book and announced loudly that I was going to read in my room. "And I'm going to lock the door," I said, "I don't want Sam and his clone barging in on me all the time."

There wasn't a lot of response, but Mum had obviously heard, so I walked very noisily up the stairs, listening out for the whereabouts of the others. Dad was back in the front room, but with the door open, dialling a number over and over again. Sam and his guest were temporarily in Sam's attic bedroom, rearranging the furniture, or possibly dismantling it. When I opened my own bedroom door I noticed the centre light was swinging in time to the thuds coming from above.

I didn't go in, though. I threw my book on the duvet, took the key from out of the inside keyhole – and then closed and locked the door from the outside. All that was easy. The only trick up to that point was to make sure the family were conveniently placed, and occupied. The next bit, I thought, was where the skill came in.

I had to get down the stairs again, undetected, past the open door of the front room and along the narrow corridor to the kitchen, passing the open door of the middle room. There is one escape hatch in this stretch – the cupboard under the stairs. I always hoped never to have to hide in there, though, because it would be so hard to explain if I was caught coming out.

The next stretch was without escape opportunities. I had to cross the kitchen, past the huge arch in the middle room, and get out of the back door without making a sound. If spotted at this stage, I used to abandon the whole plan.

If the kitchen could be crossed successfully, and the back door opened and closed under cover of sounds from the rest of the house, there was really only one awkward man-œuvre left. The back door opened onto the mouldy little side passage, and until I got myself round the corner, I could be seen from the middle room window. After that, crossing the garden was as nothing, given that I always made sure there was no one in the kitchen or bathroom, which over-looked it, before I set out.

Sometimes Henry watched me from the wall, but he'd never give me away. He's a thoughtful cat, Henry; a philo-sopher, Dad says. He's striped – you can't call him tabby, that's too undignified. Once in a while he remembers that he's supposed to have a killer instinct, and he throws himself at a bird, but he always looks relieved when it gets away.

Once I was behind the hydrangea bush, I was out of sight from all angles and could take my time sliding through the gap in the fence. The other side of the gap there was a narrow space with a tree stump in it, behind a rotting garden shed. Anyone sitting on that tree stump was protected by the shed, but could see out round it into another world.

The point is, the block I live on has terraced houses along its front and its two sides, each with a garden the size of ours at the back. We live more or less at the centre of the front terrace. Then each end of the fourth side of the block, at the back, there's a big house with a big back garden. Between these two houses, making them look a bit like lodges protecting a palace, there's a positively enormous old house, with a garage and a lean-to shed at one side of it and a conservatory in the middle. The first time I really looked at it properly, I thought it was was quite out of scale with everything else.

It wasn't the back of the house, though, that I crept through the fence to look at that day, and all those other days, it was the huge garden. From my bedroom window you could see that this garden took up almost the whole centre of the block, rather like the central gardens in London squares. Eighteen gardens like ours, plus the two bigger ones, joined onto it, divided from it by all sorts of walls and fences and hedges, and even the end of terrace gardens each touched it with one of their corners. It was as though all the smaller plots had joined hands and were dancing around it.

I didn't only love it because of its size, and because it was hidden in the middle of things. What really made it special was its richness and its patterns. The little gardens were all a mix and a muddle – one with a bird table, one with a bright blue climbing frame, one with long wild-looking grass, one with a magnolia tree which wasn't very big but which took up all of it, one full of dahlias in summer, with upturned flowerpots on sticks among them to trap the earwigs, one with roses and greenfly, all different.

The big garden, though, was planned. It had real trees – two poplars, a pine, a pink horse chestnut and three silver birches. They stood along the sides and were too tall to block anybody's light, except perhaps from one or two of the bedroom windows. The chestnut might have been a problem, but it was in the right-hand corner, if you looked at it from my stump, and so it only over-shadowed the biggish garden of the biggish house next door, which I expect could stand it.

At the end nearest to us there was a little orchard of apple and damson trees. Beyond that, moving towards the house, there was a low wall, only a foot or so high, with rock plants growing on top of it – saxifrage and aubretia. This wall was divided in the centre by two shallow, wide steps which led up to the next stage of the garden, and a great wooden pergola curved over these steps and held up an ancient rose, with such a thick gnarled stem it was almost like a small tree. In summer it was covered in heavy-looking pink flowers.

Beyond the wall was a perfect lawn with two long narrow flower beds leading from each side of the pergola up towards the house, and in summer these beds were full of forget-me-nots and snapdragons and pinks. They divided the lawn into three parts, a central strip, and two squares. A dark green conifer stood in the middle of each square, looking like a tall paintbrush, and round each one was a curved white trough on spindly legs. The troughs were filled up with variegated geraniums from the greenhouse in summer.

The reason I know the names for all these things is that Mum buys our doomed geraniums from a mail order catalogue and I've sometimes taken it into the big garden with me to work out what things are. It's easier to think about things if they have names. The stuff on the rockery, though, which is up between the house and the chestnut, was always a bit of a mystery – too far off to see properly. The other side, to the left, under the silver birches, there was a border of delphiniums and phlox and golden rod and lupins, all easy to recognise from their pictures.

Along the back of the house was a crazy-paved terrace with tubs and urns standing about on it, which would be loaded up in about a month with things I could dimly see, through distance and glass, coming along nicely in the conservatory. Finally, there was clematis and honeysuckle all up the back of the house and garage, and also holding up the shed I hid behind.

That time, that last private time, it was too early in the year for much to be flowering, but I could half see and half remember what would happen later. It was like looking at a ghost garden, but one that was haunted by the future instead of the past.

I'd often seen the owners working out there, but I made sure they never saw me. I didn't feel I was spying on them, because they must have known they could be seen from the top windows of all the houses.

They were an elderly couple, a bit bent, and they always wore gardening aprons, with big pockets, and gardening gloves. They worked very hard, but they walked very slowly, so even if one of them came down to the shed for something, I had plenty of time to get well back before they got too close.

I didn't want to be caught because not being seen was all part of the magic – but I never imagined them doing anything very drastic about it if I was.

In fact, I had two fantasies about it. In one they were so pleased I was interested in their garden that they gave me a little plot of my own in it, and I succeeded in growing something exotic there, something that had never been grown outdoors in Britain before, and then I got an important prize for it, at some big London show, and of course I was the youngest-ever winner. That was my dream fantasy.

The other was my nightmare fantasy. In that one, Sam found my secret place and brought all his friends through the hole in the fence, and the owners were distraught and boarded it up once-for-all.

The nightmare fantasy seemed the more likely to come true. I could never quite believe my luck that in almost three years Sam had never cottoned on. I suppose there were two reasons. One was that though he seemed to be everywhere, all the time, he couldn't be really. The other was that he is

6

very unobservant. One time a hot air balloon came over while we were in our little garden. The rest of us stared at it, but Sam just went on roaring around on the grass. Dad had to catch hold of him and physically tip his head back so he didn't miss the excitement. Another time there was a car crash near his school at tea-time, and half his class queued up to give the police their version of events, but Sam had been so busy revolving over the metal bar that was supposed to stop children running across the road, that his evidence was useless. He did realise *something* had happened, but his view had been so upside-down-and-backwards that he wasn't even sure of the directions the cars had been travelling in – which was the only thing the two drivers themselves agreed on.

I sat on my log and watched the crows putting the soft furnishings into the inside of their nest at the top of the pine, and I thought that however irritating it might sometimes be, Sam's unobservant nature was mainly a relief. It didn't just stop him knowing about the garden secret, it stopped him knowing about the other secret, the important one. It's not that Sam ever means to be horrible, I don't think, but I knew that if he discovered my serious secret he would be merciless. And he would certainly tell everyone.

That pair of crows had nested in the pine every year since I'd started noticing them. They kept themselves pretty much to themselves, but when Father Crow was stalking about on the lawn, I got the feeling he was the senior of all the birds. By day, anyway. I'd heard an owl, sometimes, when I woke in the night, and I expect owls take precedence over everything.

That day, I remember, I heard demon voices shrieking in the chestnut, and I watched as a magpie and a jay, who I guessed were contesting a nest site in there, exploded furiously in and out of the leaves.

The french windows of the big house opened and the elderly man, 'Mr Owner', pottered out, pulling on his gardening gloves. He set off down the garden towards the shed and I moved myself right back behind it. The battling birds weren't at all bothered and didn't break off till they were ready. Then the magpie flew to the tip of one of the silver birches and rocked itself resentfully to and fro on a twig, flicking its long tail irritably. The jay disappeared into one of the tiny gardens and I could hear it cursing through the hedge. Mr Owner reached the shed, and clattered about inside, heaving some garden tool or other out of what sounded like an untidy pile.

When the shed had been quiet for a bit, I risked looking out. He was toddling back across the garden to the rockery, with a spade over one shoulder, looking as though he'd lost his way to the film-set of a remake of Snow White. Meanwhile, his wife was coming out onto the terrace with two other people. It seemed they were getting more sociable. I didn't think they often had friends in the garden – although what with school, and swimming, and other things, they could have had weekly public barbecues without me knowing.

The visitors made me uneasy. I thought they might have sharper eyes for intruders than the Owners.

All four of them met at the near end of the rockery, where they stood and admired a shrub, almost a dwarf tree, which looked dead then, but which I knew would soon put out leaves like tiny red maple leaves.

A squirrel raced along the top of the fence to the right and stood watching them. They didn't see it. Each of its tail hairs was tipped with silver, and the sun caught on the silver tips, and it looked as though the squirrel had a sparkling halo around its sacred tail. Mr Owner began to dig a trench around the shrub and the squirrel raced on and threw itself into the chestnut and out of sight. It wasn't frightened by him, just behaving the way they always behave – urgently busy.

The shrub was obviously to be dug up and given to the

8

visiting couple to take home. I thought it must be getting too big for the rockery and I wondered what they'd plant instead.

Then there was a pause, while the spade was handed over to the visiting man for him to begin his share of the digging, and in the pause I heard Mrs Owner say – laughing a bit – "Strictly speaking, I think this is illegal." At once the other couple made a great show of turning their jacket collars up and pretending to skulk. The man even did a pantomime of leaning the spade behind him, against his own back, and then holding out his empty hands, all innocent.

They were altogether too larky, this other couple, definitely the sort who might set off unexpectedly at a brisk pace to inspect the end of the garden. I didn't want to test the dream fantasy. Reality could be different, I felt. I sidled back through the missing paling in the fence and looked at Henry, who was still lying on the side fence with one arm folded comfortably across his chest and the other hanging limply down, to match his hanging tail. He's never managed to get both arms on top of the fence at once. The odd thing is that he always manages to get both back legs on it, though you can't see how because he settles down over them and all you see are rounded striped hips.

I always felt he was on look-out for me on these occasions, because of course he knew exactly where I went – went there himself quite often – but still I had a good look round before scooting back into the house.

Later, as I was making a great noise about seeming to come out of my bedroom and stamp downstairs, I wondered why anyone should say that digging up a plant in their own garden might be illegal. It seemed an odd idea, even for a joke.

Then, as I reached the bottom of the stairs, Dad came out of the front room office saying, "I know what the trouble is, the squirrels have been chewing the telephone wires," and I forgot all about the illegal bush. I'd always thought Dad was a bit paranoid. Usually he just worries that neighbours might call on him while he's working, or that Henry will go to sleep on his desk and leave hairs on the artwork, but he'd never thought he was under attack from the garden before.

"They wouldn't do that," I said, to reassure him.

He said, "They chew anything. And if they haven't bitten it right through yet that would explain why sometimes I can make a call and sometimes I can't. And British Telecom, bless 'em, say they can't come till after Bank Holiday."

I said that nobody would answer the phone to him over Easter anyway, but I knew that wasn't much comfort because some of the people he works with seem to put in the same sort of hours he does.

He wandered into the kitchen in that way he has, as if he can't quite remember why he's doing it, and he said, "I've got all sorts of queries to chase up. If I'd known about this, I could have arranged to take the weekend off and we could have gone out somewhere."

I followed him, for something to do, but I didn't say anything. There are certain things that are known in families, without anyone ever having to talk about them, and one of the things we just 'knew' in our family was that Dad always had a rush job on that had to be finished over any Bank Holiday weekend. Another 'known' thing was that there was never any point trying to go anywhere on a Bank Holiday because everyone else would have got there first and there would be no room.

"The perils of urban living," said Dad, sadly. "I'm sure you don't get persecuted by wildlife in the country. It's all too busy avoiding traps and dogs and guns."

I said I didn't believe the squirrels had anything to do with it, and I went to the cupboard for some proper tea bags. If you leave him to it, he makes horrible watery China stuff with floating tea-leaves like torpedoes. I was sure he was wrong about the squirrels because I thought then that he was almost as unobservant as Sam, so it didn't occur to me he might have seen them at it.

He went on muttering about town wildlife, saying it had no respect for property, and that reminded me of what I'd just heard in the big garden. "Is there any reason people wouldn't be allowed to dig up one of their own plants?" I said.

"Not that I can think of," said Dad, accepting the strong tea bags without complaining. "Not unless they'd sold the house, of course."

# CHAPTER TWO

They moved out the next weekend. It was very undramatic. On Friday I noticed there were no curtains in the back windows of the big house, and on Saturday Dad came in, all pink and puffing from his run round the block, to say there was a removal van at the front of it. By Sunday it was all over.

Because it had been so undramatic, I kept forgetting it had happened, and then each time I remembered, I got cross. I couldn't think of any good reason why they should go, and also I didn't like being taken by surprise like that.

When I complained, Mum said there was no reason why they should tell anyone if they didn't want to, and Dad said the garden must have got too much for them. "You can't go on stooping and crouching over plants forever," he said, "and they must have been a good age." I said that didn't make any sense to me. They had been what he would call 'a good age' for as long as I could remember, so why should the garden be any more of a problem this year than it had been last year.

Sam bent down and jammed the top of his head on the sofa seat and said through his legs, "They shouldn't have had such a big garden in the first place. All property is theft."

There was a bit of a silence after that and then I said,

"He's heard that somewhere. He didn't think of *that* himself."

Sam flung his feet upwards, stood briefly on his head, and then hooked his legs over the back of the sofa so he was more or less hanging upside down from it. "I think of more things than you know," he said.

Dad said, "They have politics in class even at his age, these days," but Mum said, "Don't wipe your shoes on the wall."

Dad said, "I didn't even know what politics were when I was at school," and Mum said, "You still don't."

Sam, who now looked as if he was quite likely to break his neck, clapped his feet together in the air triumphantly.

I said, "You can't be politically aware when you're under four foot high."

And Sam said, "All the best things are short." He let himself sink down in slow motion until he lay in a heap on the floor in front of the sofa. "Short stories," he said, "shortbread, short cuts." He's a couple of inches smaller than anyone else in his class, and it was obvious he'd been working on his speech. I don't actually think it's fair to pick on him about it, but there are some things you can't let go. "What about short temper?" I said.

"What about short change?" said Mum, which surprised me.

"What about a short circuit?" said Dad.

Quite unworried, Sam rolled himself up into a ball, making an alarming fizzing noise, and then began to thrash his arms and legs violently, keeping them rigid. Sam Watson, the human short circuit.

It was quite effective, but I was too rattled about those two just abandoning the garden to let myself be impressed. So I told him he sounded like a bowl of cereal when the milk goes onto it.

Sam went limp and lay still with his eyes closed.

Mum looked a bit anxious. Usually the only time you get

13

a good look at Sam is when he's asleep in bed at night. The rest of the time he's upside down or spinning or running or eating or hunched up over a drawing. It was so unusual to get a mid-day freeze-frame that even I wondered for a moment if he'd hurt himself.

Then, "Too-much-milk," said Sam in a slow, slow voice with long-drawn-out words. "I've-gone-soggy."

Mum got up and went into the kitchen – she didn't want us to know she'd had a moment of doubt. We all know Sam never does hurt himself. Dad says he's made of vulcanised rubber.

Mum went to the cupboard under the sink and for some reason began to take out all the half-empty tins of paint. "Now you won't forget," she said, "that Kathleen's coming. We've only got a couple of weeks and there's a lot to do. Will someone pass me a skewer?"

"Are we having kebabs?" said Sam, walking into the kitchen backwards, for a change I suppose, and passing her one from the jar by the cooker.

"I want to see if this has all dried up," said Mum, levering the lid off a tin of white gloss and putting the skewer in like a dipstick.

I *had* forgotten Kathleen was coming, and when I looked at Dad I could see he'd forgotten, too.

The thing is – as well as the family-known-fact that Dad always works on a Bank Holiday, and that wherever you might like to go, everyone is sure to have got there first- there is also the family-known-fact that Mum and Dad don't have people to stay. They just don't. They don't have people to meals, either.

Sam or I sometimes have a friend to stay over, but that's different, and anyway we each have bunk beds in our rooms so it's easy. But there's nowhere else for anyone to sleep except the broom cupboard. There's the front room office, the middle room and the kitchen on the ground floor; Mum and Dad's bedroom, my bedroom and the bathroom on the next floor; and at the top Sam's attic bedroom and the true attic room beside it, with all the suitcases and bits and pieces no one knows what to do with. One thing this house does not have is a spare room. Well, to be accurate, it also doesn't have a swimming pool or a sauna or a billiard room, but we don't miss those, either.

The trouble with family-known-things is that they always seem peculiar if you try to explain them to anyone else. I've probably made us sound like hostile hermits who move the furniture across the front door if a stranger turns into the street, but it isn't that bad. Dad always gets on all right with everyone he works with, and Mum gets on fine with all the people who go into the shop for medicine or advice. She even knows most of them by name and what their troubles are. It's just that it doesn't go much further than that, with them. They're a bit like the crows, they keep themselves to themselves.

Then suddenly last Christmas this distant relative, Kathleen, who none of us had ever heard of before, wrote from Canada to say she was doing some research into family history. That was a bit of a shock because when we think of 'family' we just think of the four of us. Neither Mum nor Dad had brothers or sisters, and their parents died a long time ago, so we don't go in for aunts and uncles and grandparents. When there's just the four of you, all in the same house, you don't expect to have a history.

Kathleen's letter had said she wanted to spend the summer in England looking at parish records and the registers of births, marriages and deaths, and all that stuff. She had said she needed a London base, but that she wouldn't be here all the time because she'd be visiting other distant relatives all over the country, and that even when she was here, she'd be out all day.

She'd enclosed a piece of flimsy paper, folded up small, which opened out to show a huge family tree, with gaps and question marks all over the place, and her name and ours underlined in red. Mum and Dad had looked horrified. All those people! It was like an unexpected invasion of dead great aunts and second cousins and all the rest – and, what was worse, some who were still alive! They'd spread the paper out over the kitchen table and leant over it together, pointing out names to each other, and I could see they preferred the ones that had a death date written in. It isn't that there's a family feud, or anything mysterious like that – it's just that we never knew these people existed. We'd done very nicely without them up to now, and none of us much wanted to have our Christmas card lists forcibly extended.

Then Dad had said, "Well, it's your family, not mine," and had wandered back to his office, leaving Mum looking harassed – and I think that's why he forgot. He didn't feel it had anything to do with him.

Now here was Mum miserably picking the skin off dregs of paint and saying Kathleen would be here before we knew it. I would have helped with the paint but I couldn't quite see what she was trying to do. "Why didn't you tell her she couldn't come?" I said.

"How could I?" said Mum hopelessly. "She thought of everything. She said she'd be happy to sleep on the sofa, or the floor, or anywhere else. I think she'd have brought a tent and pitched it in the garden if we'd said there was no room in the house. I couldn't think of any excuse. I just hoped she'd go off the idea, but she hasn't."

"Well where *is* she going to sleep?"

"She can have my room," said Sam amiably. "I'll move in with Jo."

Before I could react to that, Mum said rapidly, "I told you – months ago – she's having the other attic."

I said it hadn't a bed, but Mum said it had. "It's got the single you slept in before we got the bunks," she said, "you probably don't remember. It's narrow, but it's full length."

I was a bit shocked. "It's a junk room," I said. However pushy someone was, however sincerely she might have offered to sleep on top of the freezer or in the bath or whatever, it didn't seem right to shove her into the junk room.

"Obviously it's got to be sorted out," said Mum, who didn't seem to like what she was finding in the paint tins. "*None* of these lids have been on properly. We'll have to get new. Now you know why I said there was a lot to do."

There was, too. All the junk in that attic room had to be shared out among the other rooms; we had to buy paint, and cheap rush matting for the floor, and material for curtains; then we had to put up with the awful smell as we did the decorating. It seemed to go on forever. Dad claims to be allergic to paint, which I thought was a bit of a cheat, but to be fair he did make the curtains. He's good at fiddly things and these were extra fiddly because of the slanting window. They had to have a wire along the bottom as well as along the top.

What with all that, and the fact that school was back again, I didn't get into the big garden for a while. I didn't even have much time to think about it; and when I looked at it every morning and evening out of my bedroom window and saw that nothing much seemed to have changed, there didn't seem to be any reason for worry.

The apple and damson trees came into bud and then into flower; bulbs came up around their feet; the silver birches put out pretty little pale leaves; the candles opened on the chestnut. It was all very comforting. Of course, I thought, plants are creatures of habit, they don't need gardeners to tell them what to do. The lawn grass did grow a little longer, it's true, but only a little, and they'd never given it its first mowing particularly early in the year anyway. You can't, Dad says, the mower just chews the new shoots like salad and leaves bits of bald earth behind.

The crows weren't bothered, either. They were obviously sitting on something in their high nest, and even from as far away as my window I could work out where the blackbirds were nesting, and the sparrows, and the blue tits and the great tits. The pair of magpies and the pair of jays had sorted out their differences for the time being, though they still kept a watch on each other out of their fierce eyes. The flight of pigeons rested as often as ever on the roof of the big house, and still flapped down into the garden several times a day, even though the bird bath on the terrace only got filled if it rained.

The sale of the house began to seem less and less important.

One afternoon, when I'd just finished my homework, Dad came in carrying a cardboard box full of unmatching cups and saucers and egg cups with feet and china frogs and other things people give you that you don't want.

"I know you took your full quota," he said, "but could you find room for these as well? It's no good putting breakables anywhere near Sam, and if anything else goes under my desk the legs won't touch the floor."

"Temporarily or forever?"

"Until the woman goes home to Canada."

"It can go under my table," I said. "As long as there's still room for my feet."

Dad put it where I said and then he came and stood beside me at the window.

"It must have broken their hearts to leave all that," he said. "Still, I expect the money cheered them up. They must have got a fortune for it, it's a magnificent place."

I was surprised. I had thought I was the only one who cared about it.

He leant his hands on the windowsill and fogged up the glass with his breath so that he had to keep moving his head to see out. "Did I ever tell you my fantasy?" he said. "That that's the Big House and all these others are servants' quarters? I'm Head Gardener."

"Really?"

"Oh yes. I always fancied redesigning it a bit. Not much,

18

it's almost perfect. It does need a pond, though."

I said perhaps that's really how it was, long ago, perhaps the gardener really did live here, or the butler or someone.

"No," said Dad, "can't have been like that really. These terraced houses are more recent. There'll have been big houses on this side, too, once, backing onto it. Then perhaps they were bombed in the war or something, or maybe they were just too expensive to keep up, and so these smaller ones were built instead."

"That one must always have been the biggest," I said. "Or at least it must always have had the biggest garden."

"I've thought about that," said Dad. "I think that whenever the big houses this side were pulled down, the owners of that house bought some of the land and extended their garden. I think the orchard part once belonged to this side. If you look at it, that makes sense. Otherwise their garden is out of all proportion."

It seemed that when Dad gazed vaguely at things, with his eyes all unfocused-looking, he really was seeing them after all. I was impressed. We both stared out of the window in silence for a bit, mentally extending our territory.

Then I said, "You don't think whoever's bought it now will change it much, do you?"

"I shouldn't think so," said Dad. "The garden must have been the major selling point. In fact, I should think it was the garden they were buying, with the house as a useful extra."

I said that was good.

"One thing that may change, though," said Dad, still staring out over the trees, "is that you may not be able to go through the fence and sit in there any more. Depends how the new people feel about it, I suppose."

If the window hadn't been closed, I think I'd have fallen out of it. "You *know* about that?" I said.

Dad looked round at me in a surprised kind of way and said, "Well, yes," as though I'd asked him if he knew this was my bedroom or something.

A memory-film began to run through my head, of all the times I'd escaped out there, all the precautions and the listening and the creeping, and all the times I'd congratulated myself on moving like a secret agent, like an American Indian tracker, like an intelligent alien getting out of hostile territory.

All I could think of to say was, "Does Mum know?"

"Well yes," said Dad in the same surprised tone. He looked at me a bit oddly for a moment and then he smiled. "But don't worry," he said, "dear old Sam, bless his thundering feet, has no idea." He stared at me. "It was only Sam you were trying to get a break from, wasn't it?" he said.

I might have lost some credibility, but I wasn't going to let go of all of it. "Yes," I said quickly, "only Sam. Though I was never sure if the old couple knew."

Right up to half a minute before I'd been absolutely certain that they did not know, but that kind of certainty was fading fast.

"Doubt it," said Dad. "Can't tell. If they did, they can't have minded. Quite likely the new owners won't mind, either, once they realise you never go further in than the old stump."

I'd often thought Dad might be a bit paranoid – now I began to think I might be catching it from him. They knew, they always had known. So what I was getting paranoid about was this – did that mean they knew the other secret as well? I thought they probably didn't, because I thought they would have said something if they did, but I couldn't be sure. I felt silly and uneasy at the same time. In case Dad noticed anything I said I was off to help with the attic painting. I was supposed to do that, anyway, as soon as I'd finished my homework.

"OK," said Dad, turning back to the window for a last look out. "Tell Mum I'll go and make some tea and bring it up."

I said, "Right," as though I had nothing on my mind but

putting emulsion on a sloping ceiling and getting drips on my hair, and I turned to go. But I had to hang around for a moment in the doorway. Threshholds were always a big problem. Glancing back, I saw Dad looking at me. He really might know. He could be daft about some things, like thinking the squirrels had cut off his telephone line, but I was beginning to realise he wasn't daft about everything. I knew I would have to be much more careful. I ran upstairs.

Before Dad could bring up the tea, the bell rang. Mum and I listened over the banisters as he opened the door. When we heard it was the telephone engineers, at long last, we left him to it.

They fixed the problem very quickly. All they did, Dad told us later, was to fit a new length of flex, where it crossed the outside back wall. When they left they gave him the old length, with the squirrels' toothmarks in it, as a souvenir.

# CHAPTER THREE

When the taxi pulled up outside, early one evening, Henry was the only one of us who didn't move, just stayed in the corner of the sofa doing his tea-cosy impression. Sam leapt to the front room window for a preview. Mum and I both stood up and then just stared at each other, as though, despite all the painting and preparation, we hadn't honestly believed Kathleen would turn up. Dad paced out into the kitchen and back again before going to the front door, saying as he went, "Prepare for an entire summer of queueing for the bathroom."

Greeting Kathleen was peculiar. Mum and Dad were very friendly and welcoming once they saw her, but whether that was because she was a relative or whether it was to hide the fact that they really didn't want her in the house, I couldn't tell. Sam went unusually quiet and just hopped about and stared.

I found I didn't know what to do. Because I'd only ever heard her first name, I hadn't expected to see someone who was definitely a bit older than Mum and Dad. She looked like a head teacher. She had on a dark brown skirt and jacket and a high necked white blouse with one of those cameo brooches at the neck with the silhouette of someone's head on it. She had a nice face and a quiet voice, and she smiled all right, but I somehow wasn't expecting the suitcases, the

22

portable typewriter, the big striped umbrella, and the three spare coats that were suddenly in our small hall along with Kathleen herself, the cab driver, and all the rest of us. Just for a moment it was as if she'd invaded us, taken us over. There seemed to be so much more of her in the hall than there was of us. Also, she insisted on greeting each of us, there and then, by name, so everyone and everything was trapped and we couldn't get control of it and move it somewhere else.

I felt almost panicky for a moment. All this had been rolling towards us since Christmas and even Mum and Dad hadn't been able to stop it. Now here it was, and it wouldn't go away for weeks and weeks.

Then we did get to grips with it. The cab driver was paid and waved off. Kathleen and Mum and Dad carried all her things upstairs. I switched off my smile and went through to the middle room.

"It's going to look like a junk room again up there," said Sam, following me. "I bet the rail collapses!"

We'd got the rail by mail order. It was tubular steel on a tubular steel frame, with feet. It came in bits and we'd put it together and set it up as close to the attic wall as the sloping ceiling would let us. It was the nearest thing to a wardrobe we could offer Kathleen, and as it had already fallen down twice, with nothing on it at all, I thought it quite likely it would do it again. But to Sam I said I was quite sure it wouldn't.

"I bet she's got those cases stuffed with relatives," said Sam. "When she opens them, people'll fall out and swell up, like inflatable dinghies. Did you see that brooch? I bet that's a shrunken relative's head."

I said, "I've always thought it was a mistake to let you stay up for the late night horror movie at weekends."

"And if she sits up in bed suddenly," said Sam, "she'll stove her head in on the ceiling." He mimed the gruesome impact, with accompanying crunching sound-effects, and then loped around the room with his shoulders hunched up to his ears. "It's perfectly all right," he said in a high voice, "I like it with my head bashed into my chest. It saves time in the mornings because I don't have a neck to wash."

"You haven't stoved your head in," I said, "and you sleep in the top bunk."

"In the middle of the room, though," said Sam, "under the high pointed bit. Her bed's in the corner."

There was a far distant rattling clatter from two floors up.

"There goes the rail!" yelled Sam. "The head goes next."

The head was still in the usual place, though, when Kathleen and Mum and Dad came downstairs again and we all sat round with cups of tea – apart from the one of us who had a Coke.

Kathleen had brought an enormous box of chocolates which she opened and put on the little table beside the TV, on top of the *Radio* and *TV Times*.

"I do hope you're not all on diets," she said. "It'll be easier to choose something more suitable when I know you better, but I couldn't arrive empty handed – especially as I have rather forced myself on you."

"Chocolates are very nice," said Mum. "But there was no need – SAM!"

"Pass them round, Sam," said Dad quickly.

"Remember we eat in an hour," said Mum, and she frowned at me as I chose a nut cluster, but I pretended not to see. I felt more cheerful. I'd forgotten that visitors mean presents, and it had sounded as though there would be more.

"I was just so eager to pursue my researches over here," said Kathleen, taking a chocolate but not eating it at once, "and your English hotel prices are simply prohibitive. But naturally I expect to pay the cost of my keep."

Mum and Dad made all sorts of grunts and gestures to show that they didn't want any money or even any mention of it, but they didn't say anything. I think they'd worn themselves out with all that smiling and greeting and hadn't yet got their strength back. Sam and I ate chocolate, and we didn't say anything, either. So Kathleen talked on, in her quiet teacher's voice, sitting right on the edge of the sofa, with her chocolate beginning to melt a little between her finger and thumb.

"It must have been awful," she said to Mum, "to be written to by an unknown relative out of the blue. You see, how it comes about is that you and I share a great-grandmother, Marion Bartlett. You come down by way of her eldest daughter, and I'm descended from the second daughter – so of course the surnames are not the same, not even our unmarried names."

At last she put the chocolate in her mouth, and then had to lick her fingers. There was no particular response from any of us, so when the chocolate was done with she said, "I was casting around for living descendants, from any branch of the family, and you're the only ones, it turned out, who live in London. So many of the important records are held here – of families who originated in Britain, that is."

Dad sighed.

"And though we don't share Marion Bartlett's surname," said Kathleen to Mum, "we do have her Christian name. It's really fascinating, when you begin to get involved in family trees, how little variety there can be in Christian names. I'm Kathleen Marion, after my mother, and I'm sure the Marion was in honour of great-grandmother Marion. And I know that your middle name is Marion, too."

"Yes, it is," said Mum, and she looked a bit indignant, I thought. It did seem odd, I suppose. You don't expect to be told your own name by someone else – you expect to tell them.

"My middle name's Marion, too," I said, in case Kathleen's researches had stopped short at Mum.

"There!" said Kathleen. "See how linked we all are really. All named in honour of one woman."

"Joanna gets her middle name from me," said Mum firmly.

"You're only interested in the female line, then?" said Dad.

"Oh no," said Kathleen, finding a hanky up her sleeve and wiping her fingers on it. "It's just that we happen to be related through the female line."

She smiled at me, pushed the hanky back up her sleeve, and passed the chocolate box to me and Sam again. "You seem to be neater eaters than I am," she said.

She turned back to Dad. "I'm really trying to link all 'our' Bartletts into one big tree," she said. "There are some Canadian cousins who are very keen, and I'm in touch with some people in Australia as well as with several outposts of the family scattered in Britain – but it's quite a common name, so it's not too easy. Sometimes I think I'm on to something, and I follow a line back, and then I find I'm pursuing a completely different lot of Bartletts."

"All in the hope of discovering you're descended from Royalty, I take it," said Dad, smiling sadly at her.

Sam, who was rocking to and fro astride the arm of Dad's chair, with a thin streak of chocolate moving slowly down his chin, stopped to listen to that, but Kathleen just laughed. "No, no blue blood," she said. "We were mostly clothiers, engineers and shoemakers, with one or two doctors from time to time. Have you ever tried to trace your ancestors?"

"I may when I retire, perhaps," said Dad. He said it very nicely, but I'm sure Kathleen knew that what he was really saying was that he couldn't imagine that he'd ever be so desperate for something to do.

"Forgive me," said Kathleen, "but I don't really know anything much about any of you – not even about your work."

That didn't cheer Dad up. He always says doing the work is bad enough, he doesn't want to talk about it as well. But of course he had to answer. "I freelance, for a few pub-

26

lishers. Designing books, seeing the production through."
Then he put his hand out to Mum, as though introducing
her onto a stage, and said, "Your relative here is a chemist, a
pharmacist I should say, based in a shop in the High Street."

But Kathleen was looking at him with an anxious expression. "Oh, so you work at home," she said, as if that explained something to her. "Oh, please don't be afraid I shall
disrupt things. I'll be out quite a lot and away quite often,
and when I am in, I shall need to spend quite a lot of time
typing up notes and letters in my room – that is, in the room
you're letting me use. I really shan't be a nuisance."

Dad smiled, but it was only his second best smile, and
suddenly I couldn't bear the way they all looked any more.
Kathleen looked apologetic, and Mum and Dad as though
they were bravely preparing to put up with the worst. Also,
the chocolates were beginning to do things to me. I needed
to be in the big garden.

I got up. "I'm going to read in my room," I said.

Everyone must have been waiting for someone else to
make a move, because they all got up as well, very quickly,
as if a bell had rung or something.

"I shall go wash-up," said Kathleen. "Maybe unpack."

"I must get the meal going," said Mum.

"I'll just go and tidy my desk," said Dad, "if you'll excuse
me."

Only Henry and Sam were unaware of the tension in the
room. Henry jumped easily onto the windowsill and sat
staring at a blackbird which was sitting in his place on next
door's fence. He moved his long striped tail very gently and
he chattered threats against the window pane. Sam followed
Kathleen out of the room saying, "I've got a space station
set out on my floor. You can come and see it if you like."

I just made for my tree stump. I'd said the bit about
reading in my room out of habit. Mum and Dad knew
where I went, Kathleen wouldn't care, and Sam's attic window pointed at the sky. He can only see into the gardens if

he stands on a chair, and I couldn't imagine him bothering, especially not if he was extending his Lego skylab.

I sat in my place half behind the shed, in the late evening sun, and I scuffed my feet in the earth and weeds all around it. They never had weeded right down at this end, and in the summer nettles always came up, and there were butter-flies.

I hoped that by the time I went indoors again everyone would have settled down a bit and accepted Kathleen. The trouble was, I think, that we hadn't really talked about her enough before she turned up.

We'd either forgotten her or pretended she'd change her mind. What we should have done, I could see when it was too late, was to talk about how awful she'd be, how pushy, what a nuisance, how she'd be in the house all the time, getting in everyone's way. Then we could have been looking at each other just now, kind of signalling to each other behind her back that she really wasn't as bad as that after all, that in fact she seemed quite nice.

It was odd, I thought, how you could watch a moment coming towards you for months and still play it wrong.

Someone in one of the little gardens to the left was putting out crumbs. The pigeons spotted their opportunity from the roof, where they always cluster, beside one of the chimneys. First one went down over the wall and out of sight, and then the rest followed it. Most of them were grey with turquoise, mauve and white neckbands, but one was a beautiful pinkish brown.

Then a crow called out a harsh message from its high nest and just after that I saw the other crow land on the wall beside the orchard and look down with one eye at where I knew the pigeons must be. It flopped over the wall to join them, and a few seconds later it came back with a crust in its beak and flew with it to the top of the pine. It must be awful to be a young crow and find you've got parents who always sound furious. Perhaps they always are furious. I don't see how you could ever say anything pleasant in a voice like that.

The longer I sat there, the more birds I could see. It may have been because they went into hiding when I first appeared and then came out again when I sat still – but I don't think so. They were so used to all of us in our gardens, I don't think they'd bother to hide. I think it was just that I got my eye in.

There was a family of sparrows on the grass among the apple and damson trees, not far from me. The three babies were almost as big as the parents, but their feathers were fluffier and they still had their pale baby beaks. The parents had hard-looking brown bills, but the babies' beaks were more like mouths – wide, pale, sorrowful mouths that turned down at the corners. They were all following the parent birds about, screaming for food and fluttering their wings as if they were dying of hunger. The parents, though, were pecking about in the grass and completely ignoring them. At first I couldn't understand this any more than the babies could, but then we all got the message. It was make-your-own-way-in-the-world time.

After a bit, the babies had a go at pecking for themselves, and though they made some mistakes at first, and flung a few useless bits of earth or leaf down in disgust, they began to get the idea. Occasionally one of the adults would stuff a bit of food absent-mindedly into one of the spongy beaks, but whether that was to encourage them or just because they'd forgotten they'd retired, I didn't know.

They were working their way closer and closer to me, but I couldn't quite see what they were getting – insects, or grass seeds, or crumbs that had come over the wall where the pigeons were eating, I supposed. Whatever it was, it wasn't long before two of the babies were getting as much of it as their parents – but the third was in trouble. It wasn't that he was lazy, he was trying really hard, it was just that he couldn't understand what it was he was supposed to eat. He pecked enthusiastically at everything in sight, but somehow he never got hold of any food. He tried fallen petals, he tried tiny stones, he even had a go at a minute bit of twig. He had high hopes for that and he picked it up three times before he finally gave up on it.

I heard Mum calling me for supper, but I couldn't just go and not know what became of him. Especially as I knew they were supposed to eat last thing at night so the food would see them through to dawn, and the sun was very low – right down to where the pine tree meets the wall.

You might not think a sparrow could have an expression, but this one did and it wasn't just on his face, either, it was all over him. First he looked puzzled, then he looked cross, then he began to get frantic. What was so sad was that he was doing all the right things – he kept close to his parents, he watched them pecking away at some wonderful feast, then he copied what they did, but it just didn't work for him. Like me, he couldn't see what they were getting. He knew how to pick stuff up, I think he even knew how to swallow it, he just didn't know how to choose it in the first place. The outside corners of his beak seemed to be turning further and further down.

I got involved in a fantasy in which I caught him and took him home and kept him in a cage, just for a week or so, feeding him with tweezers, and then I taught him to fend for himself, and at last released him into the garden. Naturally, he grew to be a large, robust bird, found a female, raised chicks and brought them all to my windowsill to show them to me in gratitude. Then I realised that if the adult sparrows couldn't teach him to eat it was unlikely that I'd be able to, and the fantasy collapsed the way they usually do. I decided to go indoors and get some bread in the hope that that might be easier for him to recognise.

Then, just before I got around to standing up, he hit on a technique. He stopped glaring hopelessly into the grass and he closed in on his mother again. As she picked up her next beakful, he shoulder-barged her and pinched it – and she let him. Then he had a go at one of the other babies, but that was a mistake, it fought back and won, so he gave up on the young ones and concentrated on mugging his parents. As he rushed them, I noticed, they usually dropped what they'd got at once, so that he picked it up from the ground. Quite soon he was beginning to get stuff for himself, as well as the odd stolen beakful. He'd cracked it. Or they'd cracked it for him.

Mum called again, and I got up to go in. I felt quite worn out. I don't know what it was I liked about the garden, really. If Dad had asked me, when he first let on they knew about the hole in the fence, I'd have said I went there because it was peaceful – but in fact, if I'm honest, it was just as ferocious and full of tensions as anywhere else.

As I pushed back past the hydrangea I began to be aware of the side effects of the chocolate. So far the problem seemed to be limited to my arms, under the long sleeves of my shirt, and to my waist. Nothing, yet, that Sam could spot. Mum and Dad might recognise some signs, though, and what would Kathleen think! I tugged my sleeves firmly down at the wrists and willed the thing not to appear outside my clothes.

My will-power held out until the shepherd's pie had been eaten and the dishes cleared, but then, as I reached out for an apple from the bowl in the middle of the table, I saw Sam staring at my hand. I took the apple quickly and put my hands in my lap, pretending to pick a bit of splashed food off my skirt. But Sam's voice echoed around the kitchen, as harsh as any crow.

"Aaaaaaaaaaaaaargh!" he said. "Aaaaaaaaaaaargh! Look! Just look!"

Kathleen, who was sitting next to him, leant back and stared wildly round the room. I think she thought there was a wasp.

"If you say 'Aaaaaaaaargh!' you must be dead," I said

31

curtly. "They only ever say 'Aaaaaaaargh!' in comics as they die, you know that. So you're dead! So you can't talk any more! So there!"

But even Sam the unobservant could see what was under his nose, and he leaned over the table, staring and staring, looking for more. "It's all over your hand and it's creeping up your neck!" he yelled in triumph.

"Sam, don't shout," said Mum.

"And I can say 'Aaaaaaaargh!' without being dead," said Sam, "because I'm not *in* a comic, so there to you!"

I hunched my shoulders up. "You're seeing things," I said, playing for time, though I knew the secret was out. I wondered how anyone ever kept anything to themselves, unless they lived on a desert island.

Mum just sighed and raised her eyebrows at me and shook her head. It was her code for 'I tried to warn you'. Dad looked quite sympathetic. Sam was gloating. Kathleen was dazed.

"You told me you could eat chocolate now," said Sam. "You can't! You still can't." He turned to Kathleen. "She gets red maps all over her after chocolate," he said. "Usually I eat hers."

"I'm so sorry," Kathleen began. "I wouldn't have brought it if I'd known."

It was nice of her to say that, I thought, considering she clearly had no idea what was going on, and didn't seem to be about to ask.

"Urticaria," said Mum, conspiratorially, leaning towards her. "Hives."

Kathleen looked even more dazed.

"Nettle rash. Heard of nettle rash?" said Dad helpfully.

"Oh – yes," said Kathleen, light dawning.

Mum leaned across and took hold of my nearest arm, as if it was a piece of furniture. She undid the cuff button on my shirt and pushed up my sleeve. There were small red blotches on the back of my hand, like insect bites, but further up my arm they had spread and joined forces until I had one huge red swollen patch which took up almost the whole of my arm from wrist to elbow. It vaguely resembled a relief map of Italy.

"Is it painful?" said Kathleen sympathetically.

"It's hot," I said. "And it prickles." I undid the top button of my shirt and opened it out a little. Since Kathleen now knew the awful truth it was almost a relief to make it fully public. Also, it itched more where the material touched it. I knew there was a large red blotch on my shoulder. I couldn't see it, but I could feel that it was working its way up my neck.

"India!" said Sam. "Pull your shirt back a bit, I want to see if Sri Lanka's coming yet." He reached out across the table, but Mum slapped his hand back. "Leave her alone," she said. "Joanna, go and take your pill. Get into your dressing gown and I'll put some calamine on you. I'm sure Kathleen won't mind."

"Oh, I am so sorry," said Kathleen. "Chocolate seemed the easy answer, but if only I'd been more imaginative with presents this would never have happened."

"I didn't have to eat them," I said. "I know I'm allergic." I felt really sorry for her. She was trying so hard, and I could see her thinking that up to now she'd got everything wrong. "Sometimes," I said, "it happens when I haven't even *seen* any chocolate."

"Go on up," said Mum.

I asked if I could finish my apple first, but that was a mistake because it kept me in the room with Sam.

"Trust you!" he said, full of energy now he'd stopped being shy of Kathleen. "I bet no one else in the world gets something like that."

"In fact, it's quite common," said Mum.

"Yuck!" said Sam. "It makes me feel sick."

"Don't be silly," said Mum sharply. When Sam says he feels sick he quite often goes into a noisy simulation which makes everyone else feel the same way.

"I may be short, but you look as if you've got the plague," said Sam.

I was annoyed to find I was a bit tearful. I said, "Don't look at me, then."

Sam said, "I can't help it."

I said, "You'll just have to control yourself."

Dad said, "Let's change the subject."

Sam said, "If it closed up all over you, we wouldn't recognise you. You could go missing and we wouldn't be able to identify you, they'd have to take your fingerprints."

"Can we please talk about something else," said Dad, in his weariest voice.

I was the one he was trying to protect, but I was the one who couldn't let it drop. I could feel my mouth going into the same sulky shape as the sparrows' sorrowful beaks. "It's not fair," I said. "I used to be able to eat chocolate without coming out in horrible red blobs. Why can't I now?"

"Come to think of it," said Dad, "I can change the subject myself." He reached round behind him to the built-in dresser and the pile of bills and notes and pamphlets that lies in a corner of the first shelf, behind the mug tree. "We had this, this morning. I forgot."

He had a brown envelope in his hand, already opened. He took out a sheet of paper, some sort of letter, and handed it to Mum. While she read it, he said to the rest of us. "The big house and garden at the back has been bought by a property developer. They've applied for planning permission, and that letter's from the Council, asking neighbours if we object. They want to pull down the house and put up a block of flats, and they want to build eight three-storey houses in the garden."

# CHAPTER FOUR

That letter from the Council gave me such a shock that I didn't say anything about it at all at first. Dad had been right when he had said that whoever had bought the big house was probably really buying the garden. What neither of us had realised, though, was that it was the land the buyer was after, not the garden itself, not the trees and flowers and little walls, not the orchard or the pergola or the rockery with its fat, fuzzy, low-growing plants.

I took my pill and Mum dabbed me with calamine and then I really did go and sit in my room and read. That evening the blobs didn't seem to go as quickly as they usually did. The patches on my hand and arm faded away, but the weals on my neck stayed where they were and my stomach grew a whole atlas of relief maps. I loosened the tie of my dressing gown, because it was itchy where it pressed on the red patches, and I decided that as I hadn't had any more chocolate I must be allergic to bad news.

For the rest of the evening I mostly just looked out of my bedroom window. The garden was so real, so full of various things, so old; I couldn't imagine it with a big block of flats and several houses standing on it. The earth would be covered over and suffocated. The worms and grubs would be buried under concrete so there would be nothing for the birds to eat. There wouldn't be room for trees or bushes, so there'd be nowhere for nests, and the butterflies wouldn't come any more, nor the bees. Some things might move into our little gardens, but there wouldn't be room for much. There wouldn't be anywhere for the crows and I couldn't believe the owls would stay, or the squirrels. It would be as if a great concrete foot came out of the sky and stamped down on everything that was nice. People going past in the roads outside wouldn't know the difference – it would all be hidden by our rows of houses. That made it seem worse, as if they were doing something so evil it had to be secret – destroying the heart of something without changing its outside, so no one would notice or care.

I think I half expected to see workmen appear on the lawn right away and start to put up brick walls. Or would they dig foundations first? I didn't know. I'd seen plenty of building sites, but they'd always looked like building sites from the time I'd first noticed them. I'd never seen a normal house and garden turned into one.

I got out my latest diary, a blue hard-backed exercise book, and I sat on the edge of the bottom bunk with the book open on my lap. I knew a diary was supposed to be a place for private thoughts, but I also knew that Sam might, just might, one day find it, so I wrote in it as though he was hanging over my shoulder, breathing on every page.

'Intrusion of Unknown Relative', I wrote. Then 'Loss of Eternal Garden'. I thought about that for a bit, wondering if you could say something was eternal when it was about to be done away with. Then I crossed out the second headline and wrote 'Loss of Garden Thought to be Eternal'. Then 'Body Still Being Unreasonable'. These headlines were meant to start me off, and my plan was that I would write the article that belonged to the headline later on. I don't think I ever did get round to that, though.

Sitting on the bottom bunk, all I could see out of the window was the tops of the trees. The high crow's nest looked out of proportion from that angle, too big, so big I could almost convince myself it was a vulture's nest. If rooks build high, it's supposed to be the sign of a good summer. I wondered if a crow building high meant the same thing. But then rooks and crows always do build high, so I guessed that most likely it didn't mean anything at all.

I pulled open the dressing-gown and looked at the red interconnecting blobs all over my stomach. They looked less like maps by then, more as if my skin had been quilted. Luckily it hurt to scratch, so I wasn't tempted.

The things your body can do to you! The first fright mine gave me was when I was about eight and my teeth began to fall out. But then new ones grew in their places, and I more or less forgot about it. The next stage, which lasted for a couple of years at least, was a lot of sneezing and hay fever. Later my body seemed to get bored with that, as well, and this year it was producing stomach pains and these awful inconvenient blobs which I couldn't pretend weren't there. They were the worst so far, I thought, because they were the most embarrassing. Anyone might sneeze, and people are used to eight-year-olds spitting and lisping through gaps in their teeth, but the blobs really did look as though they might be some dreadful disease. Sam was the only one who actually *said* "Yuck!", but other people probably thought it, privately.

And that wasn't all. I wrapped the dressing gown around me again and wrote, on the same page, 'IT Is Getting Worse'. I somehow felt I had to put that down, because it was true, and also because I thought that if I admitted it somewhere, I might get control of it. If Sam did find the diary he would just think I meant the blobs, because it seemed to be true about them, too.

In a funny way all Sam's yelling about the blobs had been quite reassuring. It reminded me that he doesn't keep nasty discoveries about me to himself. If he had noticed the other thing, he would have announced it all right. Therefore, he hadn't noticed. Maybe the blobs actually took attention away from the other thing. Maybe I put out the blobs the way an octopus squirts out ink, to hide what it's really up to.

That night I had a dream about bulldozers and I woke up in the morning with a terrible jump. I'd been so busy thinking about them building out at the back, I'd quite forgotten they'd have to destroy first.

I got out of bed and looked out of the window and everything seemed just as usual. It was sunny and clear and there didn't seem to be any wind. Father Crow was loping across the big house lawn; the jays were shrieking around in the chestnut; a squirrel raced across behind the pergola carrying something in its mouth that just might have been its baby, I couldn't see from that distance.

All the little gardens that surrounded the big one looked the same as ever, too. I supposed that everyone else, in all the little terraced houses and in the two bigger houses, would have had the same letter we'd had. I wondered why they weren't all out there, talking over their garden walls – painting banners – tying themselves to trees – protesting. Come to that, why wasn't I? Before I had time to feel guilty about that, though, the scramble to get to school and work began and I stopped thinking about it for a while.

Kathleen, I noticed, had got up early and finished with the bathroom long before anyone else wanted it. She had also made herself some tea and taken it back up to her room. I could tell that Mum was a bit put out to discover the kitchen had been used – even if only slightly used – by a stranger – but I think she must have been relieved not to have to make polite conversation through the chaos of family breakfast.

Kathleen didn't appear before I went to school, and when I got home again and went into Dad's office, he said she'd gone out not long after the rest of us and wasn't in yet. I hoped she really did want to be somewhere else all that time and wasn't just keeping out of our way. Looking back I could see that our welcome had started off quite well – for about three and half minutes – and had then more or less blown up on the launch-pad.

I often go into Dad's office before starting on homework. He always pretends he wants to be left alone till about six, but he's alone all day and I think he must need a bit of company by fourish, to see him through. That day he was trying to finish a paste-up of a book called *Do-It-Yourself Home Maintenance*. The pictures and diagrams were all in place, and he was cutting up pieces of printed text, from long galley proofs, and sticking them in place, muttering that the text was too long as always.

"Everyone will have had that letter we had, won't they?" I said, leaning against his huge work table to watch him. "The one about Planning Permission?"

Dad said that they would. He was standing up, bending over what he was doing. I noticed he was wearing his chewed-up grey sweater, the one he puts on when he's expecting a job to be difficult.

I said, "Well, will they do anything?"

"Like what?" said Dad. He wasn't really listening. He was putting the chunks of text in place, laying them down carefully, holding his breath, not yet sticking them until he'd got them just right. I could see that the last chunk over-lapped the line that marked the end of the page.

"Well, will they complain?" I said, spelling it out for him. "Protest. Do something to stop it happening?"

Dad stood upright. Then he moved a little away from what he'd done, shunting me aside. He didn't really need to move at all, he was just making the point that he thought I was in his way. "Shouldn't think so," he said. He reached out for a pad which was on the table, half behind me, and he wrote 'Cut two lines'.

"Why 'cut two lines'?" I said.

"It's two lines over," said Dad gloomily. He began to paste the bits of text in their place.

"Why not stick those two lines on the next page?" I said,

thinking that if I helped sort out his problem he might listen to mine.

"Because this page is about 'Preparing Your Plumbing for a Hard Winter,' and the next page is about 'Caring for your Outdoor Woodwork'," said Dad. "Someone's just going to have to cut two lines."

"Why don't you?"

"You can't just lop off the last two lines and let a sentence end in mid-air," said Dad, rattily. I knew he wasn't really as cross as he sounded, just concentrating. "The editor or writer's going to have to go through it and find two lines they don't need – to make space to take these two back. They won't like it. They don't like it when it falls short, either, and they've got to write extra lines to fill in."

"I still think you could do it," I said. I could understand why those two lines hanging over the edge were irritating him. I thought he might cheer up and talk to me if he got rid of them.

"*I* can't do it," said Dad indignantly. "That would mean I'd have to read it!"

I thought maybe it was the smell of the glue that was making him cross – I hate it, it gives you a headache. "What are you going to say to the Council?" I said, deciding to stop humouring him and go for the direct approach.

"Me?" he said. "Nothing."

"But you *like* the garden," I said. "You pretend you work in it. You told me."

He'd finished his page, and he picked up the next galley and stared at it, holding it stretched out away from him, one hand at the top and one at the bottom, so that it looked as if he was reading from an ancient scroll. "Jo," he said, "do you have homework to do? I don't mean to be unfriendly, but I have to finish this paste-up tonight so I can phone through the cuts and fills tomorrow, and I don't want to work till midnight."

"Just tell me," I said, "why you're not going to say

anything to the Council?"

"Because there isn't any point," said Dad. "These things happen. You can't stop progress. I agree it's sad, but we just have to get used to the idea."

"But the Council wrote to ask if we object," I said, "and we do, so why aren't we going to tell them so?"

"Joanna, that letter means *nothing*," said Dad, and he put the galley down with a draughty flourish and leant on it with one hand. "It's no more than a statement of intent. It's a formality. By law they have to ask us, but they're not going to listen to what we say. *Developers* have bought the site – don't you know what that means? It means big business, big money. They'll have paid a bomb for it and they'll be planning to make an even bigger bomb when they've built all the houses and flats and sold them. They're not going to be stopped by anything we say."

I felt sure he was missing the point. Even though he was making a big thing about looking at me and not looking at his paste-up, I knew which of us his mind was really on. "They've asked for Planning *Permission*," I said, in the same annoyingly patient voice he'd been using to me. "If you ask for *permission* that means someone could say no. The Council must be able to say no."

"They could," said Dad, speaking even more slowly, even more 'patiently'. If anyone had heard us from outside the door I think they'd have thought our batteries were running down. "But they have to have a good reason. Us not wanting it is not a good reason. We've got our own houses and gardens, no one's taking those away. Joanna, you can't stop developers – they're motivated by greed and that is one of the strongest motivations there is."

"We could try," I said, but Dad shook his head. "There are things you can do, and things you can't," he said. "One thing I can do is earn my living – *if* I'm allowed to. If I worked in ..."

I interrupted him, "... some big office," I said, "I

wouldn't be able to walk in and talk to you. I know. I'll go."

Mum was no more help when we sat down to eat that evening. "People need homes," she said, sloshing lasagne onto our plates. "And there's a lot of silly prejudice against developers."

"You think they're all kind and caring people, do you?" said Dad, who was eating fast, wanting to get back into the office. I felt a bit guilty. Maybe he'd have finished before supper if I'd let him.

"I think they're no nicer or nastier than anyone else," said Mum. "And they do a useful service – they provide homes and shops and offices for the rest of us."

"And they make money," said Dad, taking some more salad.

"Of course they make money," said Mum, in her sensible voice, the one she uses when someone goes into the shop panicking about a new doctor's prescription. ('Well of course it won't hurt you,' I've heard her say, 'it wouldn't have been prescribed if it was going to do you harm, now would it?') She tweezed up some lettuce with the wooden tongs and dropped it onto my plate. She thinks green leaves are the answer to everything, as long as you eat them. "We all like to make money," she said. "Are you doing that paste-up free?"

"I doubt if I make as much in a year as the average property developer makes in a week," said Dad.

"Yes, and don't you just wish you did," said Mum.

Sam meanwhile was talking cheerfully to himself, both between and during mouthfuls, and from the odd snatches I actually listened to I discovered that his chief reaction to the disaster was that he would be able to watch a JCB in action almost on his own doorstep. He was also developing a plan to rent out my bedroom window to his friends, that being the one with the best view. I comforted myself by thinking about the lock on the door.

42

"Joanna, stop fiddling with the fruit," said Mum. "Either take something or don't."

Three pairs of eyes stared at me. I managed to speed up the action of my hands and get an apple as far as my plate. Writing 'IT Is Getting Worse' in my diary last night had been an understatement.

If I made a truthful note about it tonight, I'd have to say it was getting much, much worse.

Partly to distract their attention, but only partly, I said, "Well I'm going to protest. I'm a neighbour and I don't like it and I'm going to write and say so."

"Won't do any good, m'love," said Dad, kindly. "You haven't a vote. It's unlikely the Council would listen to anyone, but they certainly wouldn't listen to someone who couldn't vote them back in next election time."

We'd finished eating and had even cleared up by the time Kathleen rang the doorbell. We nearly jumped out of our skins when we heard it, we'd almost forgotten she was around. She let Mum make her a cup of coffee, but she said she'd eaten out. "I've spent the whole day at St Katharine's House," she said, "going through the records, and when they closed I had a look round your National Theatre and Festival Hall, all that. Then I had something to eat before travelling back." She looked anxious. "I did leave a note," she said to Mum, "by the kettle. I hope you saw it."

"Oh yes, thanks," said Mum. "But please don't feel you have to stay out all the time. It's really no hardship to find one more place at the table."

"Thank you," said Kathleen. "Perhaps another evening I might ..."

"Have you found what you wanted?" said Mum.

"I've made a bit of progress," said Kathleen. "It takes a while, in these places, to familiarise yourself with procedure." I could see her looking at Mum, working out if Mum really wanted the details, and deciding that she didn't. (I've done that myself. 'Did you have a good day at school?' 'Yes, thanks.')

Dad went into his office, Mum sat at the kitchen table to write a letter, Sam lay on the floor in front of the TV. Kathleen sat down on the sofa behind him, facing the TV, holding her coffee, looking a bit uncertain. I had been going up to my room, but I could still remember what it was like going for the first time into big school, and not knowing anyone, and not knowing what to do. So I sat beside her.

Anyway, there was something I wanted to ask her.

We watched the TV for a bit and I found I didn't know how to bring the subject up, so, just to break the ice, I told her about the family's reaction to the Council's letter. She seemed pleased to be talked to. She listened to me and looked sympathetic. "If you really mind about it, I think you should do something," she said. "It would be sad if you did nothing and then regretted it later."

I explained what Dad had said, about no one listening to you if you didn't have a vote.

Kathleen said she could see what he meant. "But that doesn't necessarily mean you can't do anything," she said. "It just, perhaps, means you can't do anything directly."

"What other way is there?"

"Well – maybe you have to make other people act," she said. "There must be plenty around here who do have a vote. Perhaps you have to persuade them to protest."

I said I didn't even know them, not really. I might recognise a few of them in the street, but that was about it.

"You'll have to do something about that first, then," said Kathleen.

"But they probably all feel like my parents do."

"They might," said Kathleen. "But you don't know that. For all you know, they may feel exactly as you do. The trouble is, you see, most people are either lazy, or else involved with lots of other things. Then again, no one wants to act on their own. If you went round and gave everyone a shove – if for example you were able to tell each one that lots of the others were going to do something – you might get them all mobilised. A private army!"

I stared at the screen, where two men were chasing each other through a badly lit underground car park. It must have been a good story because Sam had shuffled forwards until his face was about a foot from the TV screen. This conservation was getting a bit demanding, I thought. I only wanted to persuade Mum and Dad to write a letter – I didn't want to raise an army. Anyway, I hadn't really wanted Kathleen's opinion on the garden, she was a foreigner and it wasn't anything to do with her. I was only making conversation because there was something else I wanted to get out of her. I tried to bring up the other subject casually. "Have you managed to go further back into the past than Marion Bartlett today?" I said.

"Oh, I'd gone a lot further back than her before I left Canada," said Kathleen. "I'm going sideways in all directions now. If you remember that everyone has two parents, and that the people they marry each have two parents, you can imagine that the thing spreads out like anything. Also, I'm trying to find out a bit more about some of them. Peasants we may be, but some of us had quite interesting lives."

That led so neatly into what I wanted to ask that I could hardly believe my luck.

"So you do find out about people?" I said. "More than just their names?"

"Oh yes," said Kathleen. "Some things are easier than others, of course. But it's usually not too hard to find out where people lived, what jobs they did. A birth certificate doesn't only tell you when people were born, but where, and also what, their parents did. Then a marriage certificate shows ..."

But I didn't want all that. "Have you discovered any madness in the family?" I said casually, staring hard at the

45

TV, speaking, I hoped, too quietly for Mum or Sam to hear what I said.

"Not yet," said Kathleen cheerfully.

"Would that kind of thing show up?"

Kathleen, who had also been staring at the TV, turned to look at me. I didn't look back at her.

"I think it would probably show up one way or another," she said. "For example, a death certificate tells you where a person died, so I'd know if anyone had actually died in a lunatic asylum. And then for the more recent ones there are the census forms – they start properly in 1801 but you're not allowed to look at them for a hundred years, so effectively they only run from 1801 to 1888, at the moment. There's a special column on each form where the head of the household was supposed to note down if any of the family were 'imbecile' or 'lunatic'. There's certainly nothing like that in the immediate family – but I'm finding more distant sections of it all the time and I haven't got very far with some of those."

She watched me all the time she was speaking. Even though I didn't look at her, I could see out of the corner of my eye that her face was turned towards me. She went on looking at me when she'd finished. I was quite sure she was waiting for me to tell her why I wanted to know – and if I didn't tell her, she was going to ask. I had to think of something quickly, to take her mind off it. I said, "If you know our family tree further back than Marion Bartlett, why did you tell us we're descended from her? Why not from her great-great grandmother, or however far back you've gone?"

"Oh," said Kathleen, and she sort of half-laughed. "I'm not sure."

I got the feeling I'd caught her out in some way, though I hadn't meant to, and I didn't know how I'd done it. She waited for a few moments, and I twitched my toes inside my shoes and wondered which of us was going to ask the next awkward question.

Then Kathleen said, "I think it was just that I wanted to try and catch your interest – all of you, that is – so I picked the person whose Christian name we all seem to carry."

"Ah," I said. I could have accepted that, that would have done nicely.

But after a moment, she went on. "No, it's more than that, if I'm honest," she said. "There's something about Marion Bartlett that's always appealed to me. She was quite an intrepid lady, you know."

"How do you mean?"

"She ran away from home when she was eighteen – this was in 1880, a time when young ladies didn't do such things. My theory is that her parents wouldn't let her marry the man she chose – or perhaps they were trying to force her to marry someone she didn't choose. I haven't been able to get to the bottom of it yet. She was highly religious and she went to Canada as a missionary. As far as we know, she set off in a group. What they were doing taking her with them and not sending her back home, I can't imagine.

"Anyhow, after a couple of years she seems to have broken loose and set off westwards on her own. She must have had a bit of money with her at first, but then later on the story goes that she travelled with no money, relying on hospitality. Instead of singing for her supper, she preached and told stories. Improving stories, I imagine. She got right up into the North West Territories – it's very remote up there even now – but then! She preached to Indians, to trappers, to lumberjacks. No one harmed her. I think in a way she might have been safer than a man would have been in the same circumstances, because she wasn't a threat, you see.

"She kept on the move, in a kind of massive circle, and worked her way back towards Ontario. I don't know if it was her plan to do that or not. There were distant relatives in Toronto, and we think she stayed with or near them. She married in Toronto, a railway engineer, and they had three children. The last one, a boy, died when he was tiny, and not long afterwards her husband died, in an accident on the railway. She came back to England after that. Lived, we believe, with her married sister and brought up her two daughters over here. The younger one, my grandmother, went back – but her sister, your great-grandmother, stayed over here. When it comes right down to it, I don't know much more about her life than that – but I feel I can imagine something of how it must have been."

"Tough!" I said.

"Tough," said Kathleen. "And downright dangerous."

I looked at Sam. He'd wriggled himself even closer to the TV so he could follow the story without our voices interrupting him. Poor old Sam, I thought, I must remember to tell him sometime that he was descended from someone who'd met Indians and lived with trappers.

"That's why I chose to follow the Bartlett line," said Kathleen. "My grandmother died when I was ten, but I can remember bits of stories she told us about her mother, about Marion."

"It's all very well," I said, "but we're not Bartletts, either of us, because we come down from her daughters – and *she* wasn't a Bartlett, either, really, she just married one."

"She was a Bartlett through and through," said Kathleen triumphantly. "You know I said she stayed with, or near, relatives in Toronto – well, they were second cousins, they were Bartletts. She was born a Bartlett and she married a Bartlett. And as for us, it's only a convention that the name comes down through the male line. We stand just as much chance of inheriting characteristics from the women in our past as from the men. In fact, Marion Bartlett's become a bit of a talisman for me."

"In what way?"

"Oh well" – Kathleen laughed a bit – "I don't really like admitting this, but I always think of her when I feel nervous.

For example, going into St Katharine's House this morning and not knowing at first how to look up the records, not really knowing what I was doing, I began to feel weak at the knees. I just wanted to take a trip on the Thames and forget the whole thing. Then!" She winked at me and stretched out her right arm and pressed the finger and thumb of her left hand onto her wrist, as if she was taking her own pulse. "I just reminded myself," she said, "that Marion Bartlett's blood flows in my veins and that going into a strange reference library is as nothing compared with braving timber wolves and blizzards."

I said I always forgot that grown-ups could get nervous, too.

"And how!" said Kathleen, rolling her eyes. "I was terrified of coming to stay here – still am. I'm not normally so pushy, forcing my way into people's homes. I just couldn't see how else to follow up the various leads which are over here."

"We are a bit frightening, I suppose," I said. "Sorry about that."

"Everybody's frightening if you don't know them," said Kathleen.

"I don't know the people around here," I said. "That's why I feel nervous about chatting them up about the garden."

Kathleen nodded quite sympathetically, and we both stared at the TV for a few more minutes, across Sam's head. I don't know if Kathleen could follow what was going on, I certainly couldn't, I'd lost the thread before I'd ever really grasped it. Then I sensed that Kathleen was looking at me again. I looked back and saw that she was feeling her own pulse, and raising her eyebrows at me.

I laughed and tapped my own wrist. "Marion Bartlett would just get on with it?" I said.

"I'm absolutely confident that Marion Bartlett would," said Kathleen.

# CHAPTER FIVE

I was sitting at the kitchen table with a blank pad and an empty mind. I could have done with some help, composing the petition, but none was on offer.

Mum seemed quite pleased that I was being so enterprising, but she refused to advise on the wording because she didn't agree with the protest.

Dad didn't exactly disagree, but since he thought it was a waste of time he left me to it – though he did say I could print it out on his word processor if I liked.

Kathleen had packed a bag and gone to visit some sort of cousins somewhere in the Midlands countryside. They were descended, she had said, from Marion Bartlett's sister, and just might have letters or papers that would fill out Marion's story a little. Also, it seemed, Marion's father's family had lived in that one area for generations, and local parish records might have all sorts of other family links.

Sam was sitting opposite me with his homework, drawing a waffle on the front of his history exercise book.

"I thought you were doing that on the word processor," he said, when I admitted what it was I was struggling with.

"It's not ready for that yet," I said.

Sam looked at me pityingly. "You're supposed to put it on the word processor from the start," he said, "and change it as you do it. That's what they're *for*." He took a silver biro out of his zip-up pencil case and began to colour in the waffle, quite carefully.

"I know what they're for," I said irritably. I wasn't prepared to explain to Sam that I didn't feel able to sit down in front of that machine without any real idea of what I wanted to say. It always looks to me as though it expects you to know what you're doing. "Why are you colouring that silver?" I said, to change the subject. "Waffles are light brown."

Sam looked at me with more scorn than I've ever seen collected on one small face before. Then he flung his arms in the air, accidentally letting go of the biro which flew across the room and hit the freezer. "Waffles!" he said. "*Waffles*! This is a portcullis!"

"Oh, well, whatever," I said, returning to my blank pad and writing 'Dear Sir' at the top, and then adding 'or Madam' to keep things fair.

"I shouldn't bother," said Sam, tipping his chair back at a dangerous angle to reach for the pen. "Who's going to take any notice of someone who can't even tell a portcullis from a waffle."

"I don't see that it matters which it is," I said, with some dignity, writing down the address of the big house, and then underlining it, by way of a heading.

"You don't see that it matters?" said Sam, outraged. "A waffle is hardly going to keep out enemy invaders, is it? *Is* it?"

"It could, if you made it of poisoned dough and they tried to eat their way in," I said, and, pleased with that bit of invention, I swept on to write three sentences explaining that the garden was large and beautiful and full of wildlife, that all the neighbours enjoyed looking at it, and that we all strongly objected to the idea of losing it. "And I don't see why you should snarl at me just because you can't draw," I said to Sam, who was still waffling on indignantly about his portcullis.

Then, in what I thought was a move of pure genius, I wrote that there was a derelict factory at the back of the new Shopping Centre, on the other side of the High Street, that would make a much better site for the new flats and houses. Feeling that a pompous final line was called for, I ended with 'I hope you will give careful consideration to our objections when considering the application for planning permission.'

"I'm going to the office," I said, walking away from the kitchen table with a nice sense of achievement.

It looked quite impressive on-screen, apart from the fact that 'consideration' and 'considering' didn't look good together. Eventually, after more thought than a single word seemed to deserve, I changed the line to 'when looking at the planning application' ... then I printed it out, and decided to give myself twenty-four hours to gloat over it before going on to the next, and far more worrying, stage.

It had crossed my mind to ask Sam to come with me on my walk around the block to ask for signatures on the petition, but as soon as I was outside the front door next evening, with my stomach revolving like a Magimix, I was glad I hadn't. He might have agreed, and there was no way that even Sam could have failed to notice my peculiar behaviour. *It* had taken a definite turn for the worse.

As I went out of the front gate, which was dangerously close to Dad's office window, I found I had to touch each gate post and the gate itself five times each, and also had to tap my right foot five times on the ground, exactly between the gateposts.

I moved slowly, to give myself time to perform this magic charm without making it too obvious, and when I'd finished I glanced back. All I could see, though, was a mixture of reflection in the glass and the outline of Dad's head and shoulders, bent low over his huge table. He hadn't even seen me go out, so he certainly hadn't seen my weird behaviour.

I can't explain what I thought that particular charm was

for, except that it had to do with getting back safely later on, mission completed.

I relaxed a bit and began to turn in at the gate next door, to the right, but then it came to me that the neighbours were more likely to be sympathetic if I touched their gateposts five times each on the way in, and also tapped five times on the path with each of my feet, not just the right foot. The neighbours mustn't see what I was doing, of course, and would never know why they felt in such a good mood as they opened the door to me.

That was how it always was. The idea of exactly what rite I should perform always just came to me, without me thinking it out. It didn't come in words, it wasn't that I heard voices, that would have been too much to bear. It was just that suddenly I would seem to know what had to be done, and always it was to do with the number five, which I regarded as magically perfect. I thought of it as a shape – a dot at each corner and one in the middle. The fact that I thought of it that way meant that I could also tap out the charm on the roof of my mouth with my tongue, a tap at each corner and one in the middle. I wasn't sure if this showed from the outside – but sometimes it came to me that I should blink five times while looking at something worrying, an unopened school report or the dentist's drill, and I knew that that did show, and that I had to be extra careful.

It could all get quite tiring, and it was very tricky if there was anyone there who might notice. They'd realise I was a bit mad, I thought, which was bad enough, but also they'd be sure to ask questions – why do you do it? – what started it? – how do you know what to do? – what would happen if you didn't do it? – and I truly didn't know any of the answers.

Sometimes the danger I was warding off was obvious – the dentist's drill wasn't hard to work out. Other times it was just that I seemed to know that harm would come to me or to someone I cared about if I didn't do whatever it was I felt

I had to do.

No one answered next door. I knew who lived there, two girls, and I knew they were out at work all day and that there wasn't much chance of catching them in straight after school like this, so I wasn't surprised. In fact, that was partly why I'd turned to the right out of our gate. The neighbours on the other side were definitely in, and I didn't feel I'd be able to cope if the very first people I called on sprang out at me.

I moved on to the next house – and I think I was punished for being such a coward, because it came to me then that the threshhold of each property ought really to be touched twenty-five times, five times five being the ultimate good number and therefore the one most likely to bring success to the petition. There was nobody in there, either, and by the time I was approaching the third house I was more or less tap-dancing in its gateway, furious with myself, scared about my sanity, but quite unable to ignore my inner instructions.

There was no response at the third house, either, which brought me to the corner one. After a brief delay there, and some scuffling in the hall which seemed to answer my scuffling on the doorstep, the door was opened by two boys of about Sam's age who said their mum was out and would not be back till later. "What about your dad?" I said, but they looked blank and went inside again. Theirs, I knew, was the garden with the bright blue climbing frame which I could see from my window if I leaned out.

I turned the corner into the narrow side road, away from the build-up of afternoon traffic. Morning and evening traffic was quite noisy and fumy in our road, which was used as a rat-run between two main roads – that's why Henry is never supposed to go outside the front door. Dad, though, says he likes it. He says that starting and ending his working day to the sound of crashing gear changes and angry horns makes him feel less cut off from normal life.

The first house I came to in the side road looked a bit

seedy, somehow. It was the same design as all the rest, but the paint on the door and gate was bubbling up, and the net curtain in the front window was either an unusual shade of mink brown or else the dirtiest white I'd ever seen in my life. There was a hole, I noticed, in this brown net curtain, to one side – and as I stood on the doorstep, with my tongue making patterns of five in my mouth, I was a bit alarmed to see a single eye watching me through it.

When I looked directly at the eye it disappeared, and shortly afterwards there came a faint shuffling from behind the front door, growing closer. I felt a strong urge to turn and walk smartly away – then I remembered I was Marion Bartlett's great-great-grand-daughter, and I stood my ground. In the end, nothing more frightening than a very old woman opened the door. She had thick white hair, cut in a raggedy shape, and she wore a flowered apron over her dress and pink feathery mules on her feet. She was quite small and very stooped, and she gave me a nice smile and said, "I'm so glad you've called, dear, could you possibly tell me the correct time?"

"Oh, yes," I said, looking at my watch, "twenty past four." Then I drew in my breath to explain about the petition, but before I could get going the old woman said, "Is that the *exact* time, dear? It is important, otherwise my wireless listening gets all messed up."

"Oh," I said, and looked back at my watch. "Well, just wait a second or two – it's just coming up to twenty-one – yes, that's it, it's exactly twenty-one minutes past four."

"Twenty-one," said the old lady nodding. "And you say your watch is reliable?" She didn't wait for an answer, but went on, "Now just wait a minute, dear, while I get *my* watch." She turned away and pottered slowly down the hall, speaking as she went. "It's too heavy to wear, I find," she said, "so I keep it on the sideboard, but I'll just fetch it and then I can set it exactly right." She disappeared into the back of the house.

I stood and waited. I thought of the view from my bed-room window and I realised this was the house with the back garden full of long wild grass. It seemed the old woman wasn't a great fan of gardens – but she looked friendly, and I thought she might sign.

When she eventually came back she was carrying a pretty gold watch on a black ribbon wrist strap. "Now then," she said, as she got closer to me, "I forget to wind it, you see, my fault entirely, and it stops, and then of course I'm lost." She held it in one hand and pulled out the winding knob gently. "Exactly twenty-one minutes past four, you said," she muttered, turning the hands.

Precision was clearly vital, so I looked at my own watch again. "Well – now it's exactly twenty-three minutes past," I said helpfully.

The old woman looked up sharply at me with a frown. "You told me twenty-one minutes past," she said accusing-ly. "Clearly and distinctly, you said twenty-one."

She looked quite different, and I took a step back. "Well, it was then," I said feebly. "You took two minutes to fetch your watch."

"Everybody is *so* unreliable these days," said the old woman, glaring at me. "Twenty-three, you're saying now, are you? But how am I to trust you when you say one thing one minute and something different the next?"

"Time passes," I said, feeling a bit helpless. Then I put out my hand. "Shall I put it right for you?" I said. That seemed the simplest answer.

But the old woman stepped smartly backwards and the nylon feathers on her mules waved about under my eyes. "If you take this, I shall call the police," she said. "I'm not afraid to be a witness."

I stepped back even further than she had, so we were now standing well away from each other. Twenty-five taps clearly hadn't been enough for this gatepost. I would have liked to go, there and then, but I didn't want to leave her in that mood. I thought she might yell after me and someone might really send for the police and they might misunderstand my motives. "I was only trying to help," I said as soothingly as I could, putting my hands behind my back. "You do it."

She looked back at her watch and her expression was quite calm again. She put her tongue out half an inch and twirled the hands of the watch slowly, slowly. Craning my neck to read the dial upside down I could see, just, when she got the hands to four twenty-three.

She looked sharply up at me again. "Now, you're not playing me false this time?" she said. "You're sure it's twenty-three minutes past."

I didn't mean to, but I looked at my own watch automatically. It was now after twenty-four minutes past. I drew a deep breath and tapped my thumb twenty-five times on the petition which I was now holding behind me. "Yes, twenty-three past," I said firmly.

She pushed the winding pin back in and smiled at me. She had a very sweet smile. "Thank you, dear," she said, and I could see she was about to close the door.

Perhaps I should have let her, but I didn't. I went forwards again and I said, "Oh, please wait," and then I launched into my 'piece' about the garden and the Council letter and the petition. Finally, I read out the petition. She watched me, smiling, and when I'd finished she said, "You want me to sign something? Of course I will. You've been so helpful about getting my watch right."

I felt a bit odd as I gave her the petition and the biro. I don't think she'd had any idea what I'd been talking about, and I wasn't sure if it was all right to let her sign something she didn't understand. But I couldn't very well stop her. She carried the thing to the hall table, and bent right down over it, and wrote her name carefully, and then brought the petition and biro back to me. "Thank you," I said.

"That's perfectly all right," said the old woman. "I'll do anything for someone who's helpful. But there was a girl here earlier who kept messing me about – one minute telling me it was twenty-one minutes past, the next moment changing her mind and saying it was twenty-three past. I wouldn't have signed anything for her, little devil."

I backed out of her gate and clicked it shut, and just as I turned into the next house, she raised her voice and called after me. "I wonder, dear," she said, "can you tell me the exact time?"

I pretended not to hear, skipped the next house and went to the one after. By the time I'd fiddled with the gate and gateposts, and rung the doorbell, the old woman had gone back inside and closed her front door. As I stood there, I knew something unfortunate was happening. One of my blobs was beginning to come up under my right eyebrow. I touched it carefully – five times – but as far as I could tell it hadn't begun to swell yet. It was just a prickly-feeling patch, and probably red.

Then the door was opened, by a youngish man, who listened to me rather crossly, I thought, and then said, "Just you wait there a minute," and stamped off into his back room leaving me hovering apprehensively on his doorstep. Despite the fact that I tapped twenty-five times with my right foot and then twenty-five times with my left, he was in no better a mood when he came back, carrying a pair of jeans.

"Look at these!" he said ferociously, holding them out.

I backed away slightly and stared blankly at the crumpled blue jeans which had some paint splatters on them.

"These were out on the line," said the man. "Clean. Next thing I know, her-next-door is chucking bread around and every bird south of Watford is flying over my garden. NOW look!"

The marks on the jeans weren't paint splatters, I realised, they were bird droppings.

"Ah," I said, not really understanding the connection with the petition.

He helped me out on that. "I wouldn't have left my perfectly good flat and come to live here if I'd known what it was going to be like," he said. "Can you imagine midsummer, when it gets light really early? They all start screaming as soon as the sun comes up, you know."

"It's the dawn chorus," I said, recovering a bit. "I like it."

"Well, I have to leave for work at seven, thank you very much," said the man, "and I need my sleep. If you want my opinion, the sooner they concrete over that garden and drive the blasted creatures somewhere else, the better. So you can stick that on your form!" He rolled the jeans up into a ball. "And these'll have to be washed again," he said. He stepped back and closed the door and I could hear his footsteps going away.

"Thanks a lot," I said to the closed door. "I think the birds have spoken for all of us."

I sidled cautiously back to the house between his and the old woman's, keeping a look-out for a roving eye-ball in the curtain hole, but no one answered the bell and the curtain hole stayed empty.

I went on to the house beyond the ruined jeans and rang that bell, hoping very much that no one was in there, either. Then Marion Bartlett said, 'That's a bit feeble of you,' and I remembered that I did really want as many signatures as possible. I just about managed to feel pleased when the door opened, though I did let myself hope that whoever was behind it wouldn't want to show me anything or ask me anything.

Quite a nice-looking woman stood there, a woman I realised I'd often seen dragging a pully-wheely basket over other people's feet in Sainsbury's. This, obviously, was the bird-feeding lady.

"I'm *absolutely* on your side, dear," said the bird lady when I'd explained, "I couldn't agree with you more, it's a tragedy."

I smiled at her.

"But," said the bird lady, "there may be a snag. I'm not sure I can sign your paper."

"Why not?" I said, and it came out as a bit of a wail.

"I'm afraid it rather depends on who else has signed," said the bird lady. She twitched her head at the house next door. "I'm afraid I can't have my name on any paper *he* signed. Living next door to him is bad enough. I'm not having my name associated with his, not anywhere."

I told her he hadn't signed. "He hates birds," I said.

"When he first moved in, he told me he bought his house just because of the garden," said the bird lady indignantly. "He said it was like living next door to a park."

"He's gone off it now," I said. "Doesn't like the singing."

"*Well*," said the bird lady. "That's how trustworthy he is. Says one thing to me and another to you. He's a roofer – I've always found them very moody types." She held out her hand. "Would you mind if I looked at the signatures? Not that I think you'd mislead me, but one has to be careful."

I handed over the petition with its single, shaky name. "I've only just started," I said, defensively.

The bird lady's face softened a bit. "Ah bless her," she said. "Did she ask you the time?"

"Yes," I said, "and I didn't manage to give it to her quite right. It kept going on."

"She is a worry," said the bird lady, signing. "But she does very well really. There you are dear. I don't suppose for a moment anyone will read it, but it's nice to know someone else cares about the garden. I've told my husband I'll have a nervous breakdown when they take it away, but I don't suppose that matters to developers. I think something's bitten you above the eye, dear, or is it a sting?"

"A mosquito, I think," I said, and I moved rapidly away.

There didn't seem to be any humans in at the next house, but a great explosion of barking came out of the letter-box, so I moved on fast. The next stop was round the corner, in the actual street where the big house stood with the smaller but still quite large houses on each side of it. The first, just round the corner, was double fronted and had a proper garden path, not like ours, with rose bushes each side of it. There was a brass plaque beside the door, with 'Dr James MacGuire and Dr Margaret MacGuire' written on it. A grey-haired woman in a tartan skirt and white shirt opened the door. "There's no surgery at the house on Wednesday," she said, rather irritably, "you'll have to go to the Health Centre."

I said my piece about the petition and she relaxed a bit. "I'm so sorry," she said, "I assumed you'd come about the urticaria. We were going to write to the Council in any case, but of course I'll sign this as well."

She handed it back and then frowned at my eye. The thing was prickling and itching right up into my eyebrow now, and it was beginning to feel sore as well, a sure sign it was swelling.

"Are you one of ours?" said Dr MacGuire.

"No I'm not, thank you for signing," I said, retreating rapidly down the drive.

Then I walked past the front door of the big house itself.

It looked sad but rather magnificent, its windows all dark and blank without curtains, and a few weeds beginning to come up in the gravel of its half-moon shaped drive. There was a wisteria, old and dark and woody, spreading over almost all of the front. Wisteria seemed a good name, the whole place looked decidedly wisteria, I thought. It also looked as though it promised a good garden at the back, but no one who hadn't seen it could possibly have known just how good. I sent a telepathic message over its roof to the trees and the crows and the rest – 'Don't worry, you lot in there' went the message, 'I'm out here, fighting for you.'

The house beyond, twin to the doctors', had three bells by the front door; flats, and they must all have belonged to people who were out at work all day, because no one answered any of the rings.

I went round the corner and began on the third side of the square, pushed on by Marion Bartlett, worn out by my ritual fives, and with the blob above my eye now so swollen I could see it sticking out at the top of my vision.

In the first house there was a cheerful West Indian man who said he hated to be unhelpful but he couldn't possibly sign. He'd had trouble enough finding a place himself, he said, and even now there were some who didn't think he and his family should have a house of their own. He couldn't sign anything that would make it harder for someone else to have a home. He sounded like Mum, and I felt depressed.

When I rang the bell at the house next to him, the door opened at once and a very smartly dressed woman sprang out and drove me backwards down the path in front of her, talking all the way, drowning out my prepared speech. "Just because I don't go out to work everyone thinks I've nothing to do with my time, which is not at all the case," she said. "I seem to be prey to every passing American missionary, double glazing salesman and political agitator who's ever been born." She had a handbag on her wrist and she was wearing a navy jacket over her navy dress, so I realised she'd been on the point of going out when I'd touched the bell.

"I suppose you're political," she said, and snatched the petition and glared at it in an unfocused kind of way. I felt very protective of my three precious signatures, and I was just about to try to take it back, when, to my amazement, she snicked open her bag, took out a classy biro, hit its top with a flick of her thumb so that the nib popped out, and signed. Just like that. "There," she said, retracting the biro nib, replacing it, closing the bag and smacking the petition back at me, all in about two seconds. Then she clonked off briskly down the road.

By now the swelling under my eyebrow had extended itself downwards on to my eyelid and I was having to tip my head back to see out of that eye at all. The smart, efficient

# Chapter Five

woman had been too busy with her flicking and clicking and snapping to notice, but the next door was opened by a youngish woman with a sticky baby, and she kept glancing at my eye all the time I was explaining.

"How did you do that?" she said, when I'd finished, pointing at it with her free hand. Her other hand was supporting the baby, which also stared at me, with one finger up its nose.

"Oh – it swells sometimes – it's nothing," I said. "Will you sign?"

"It's a bruise, isn't it?" said the woman.

"No," I said. "I'm just allergic to things. Do you agree about the garden?"

"Where do you live?" said the woman.

She had looked perfectly nice and ordinary when she'd opened the door; I couldn't think why she was being so unreasonable. I told her where I lived, and I held out the petition with one hand and my biro with the other.

"Are you one of a big family?" said the woman.

This signature obviously had to be worked for. I told her about Mum and Dad and Sam – and I tapped out patterns of five on the paper with the biro, quite subtly I thought, hoping to speed her up.

The baby took its finger out of its nostril and lurched forward in her arms, stretching the finger out towards me. I backed discreetly.

"I expect your family is quite strict with you, aren't they?" said the woman.

I tried to give her an encouraging look out of my best eye, the other one having closed completely by then. "They don't agree with the petition," I said, "but they don't mind me doing it. Would you like me to hold the baby while you sign?" Marion Bartlett must have come up with that idea, I decided. It looked a nice enough baby, but I remembered Sam at that stage, and the awfulness that sometimes gushed out of either end without warning.

"I'll tell you what," said the woman, "I'll come round to your house later this evening, and sign. My husband can have the baby. I'll only come for a few minutes. That'll be all right, won't it?"

I couldn't think of any good reason to say no, so I said yes, and went on to the next door, wondering why people couldn't just stick their names down and have done with it.

In the next house a woman in a red and gold sari said she didn't know what to do, she didn't want to go against the wishes of the neighbours. After long negotiations, she agreed that if the final total of signatures numbered more than half the people on the block, I could come back and she'd add hers. The way things were going, I thought it was unlikely she'd see me again.

There was no reply next to her, and then in the corner house a man with enormous eyebrows signed briskly, saying, "Just come down our road, have you? It's like a foreign country these days. If they build out the back I suppose we'll get even more of them."

I stared at his signature for a while after he'd gone in and shut the door, and I didn't like the look of it at all. But it was there now, and I desperately needed to make up numbers. I decided to try and pretend to myself that I didn't know what he'd meant.

His neighbours were out, and that brought me to the final door in the circuit, our next door neighbours, the ones Dad calls The Fusspots. They came to their door, as they always did, more or less together, one behind the other, and spent ages snuffling over the paper like little grey hamsters, telling each other who they thought the signatures belonged to. "Climbing frame hasn't signed, I see. That'll be the rose garden, doctor it says, didn't know he was a doctor, must be in private medicine, house like that. Dahlias has signed, look, that's Dahlias, I'm sure."

When they'd enjoyed themselves, they passed the paper back to me saying that they certainly weren't going to put their names to something that my own parents 'didn't see fit to sign', and that they were surprised at me for thinking they would.

I tottered indoors, sat alone at the kitchen table, and tapped everything within reach twenty-five times each, in case that should improve my total. Then I counted up the signatures. It didn't take long. The hour and a half of anxiety and confusion had brought in just five of them, and two possibles. Well, Marion Bartlett, I thought, I did try.

# CHAPTER SIX

The woman with the baby – Sarah – did come round, though without her baby, and she did sign – eventually. The weird thing was, it turned out that she and Henry were already friends.

"He often comes in our garden," she said, stroking him. "We've always called him Tiger. I could never work out where he lived, but I could see he had a good home."

She didn't stroke him the way we do, all down his back, she just rubbed the top of his head, really hard, so that his eyes were forced half shut and his head nodded up and down. I wanted to tell her she was doing it all wrong, but I couldn't very well, because he loved it, purred until he made himself cough. I had thought I knew all about Henry's life – it was a strange feeling to find that he knew people we didn't.

The reason Sarah didn't sign at once was because it turned out there was an embarrassing misunderstanding to be cleared up first. She came in and sat at the kitchen table and drank tea with us, while everything was sorted out, which meant we ate later than usual that evening. This was not appreciated. Mum and Dad hate to have their routine disrupted.

When Sarah finally bent over the petition with a biro in her hand she recognised the name of the Dahlia man in the corner house and said she was specially pleased to sign next to him because he'd be so annoyed if he knew.

"Three times, now, he's asked me why I don't go back where I came from," she said. "I'm sure it's Jamaica he has in mind – I haven't the heart to tell him I'm from Peckham."

Just as she was going she said, "By the way, my husband said to tell you there was a big petition got up about five years ago, to save that Georgian house three blocks down the main road, you know the one? It's solicitors' offices now, I think. He says the Council declared a Conservation Area, or something, because there are one or two other nice houses and some big trees around, and he's sure this block comes into it. So we shouldn't have too much to worry about."

"I have a feeling," said Mum, when she came back from seeing her out of the front door, "that this petition is going to turn out to be more trouble than it's worth."

"It already has," said Dad, who was still sitting at the table, looking a bit dazed.

Sam, fortunately, was over at a friend's house, so there were only two pairs of eyes to glare at me.

"She signed, though," I said, hastily, "and she told us that thing her husband said. I liked her. Henry likes her."

"We all liked her," said Mum, "that's not the point. You do realise, don't you, why she insisted on coming to the house to sign? You do realise she wanted to get a look at us?"

"At me," said Dad, and he looked seriously depressed, not just his usual depressed, "it was me she suspected."

I could understand it had been a real shock to him to realise that someone actually thought he'd punched me in the eye. It had come as a shock to me, too. Not that Sarah had said in so many words that that was what she thought – she'd just kept looking at all of us, and looking round the kitchen, and talking about the swelling. Then gradually she'd got friendlier as she began to believe I wasn't a battered baby after all.

"We put her right, though, didn't we?" I said encouragingly. "It was fine once we pointed out the urticaria and started explaining about it – and it was great the way the eye swelling went down right in front of her. And then when this one inside my elbow started to come up, it was brilliant. You have to admit that was brilliant. That really convinced her."

"As ways of passing the time go," said Dad, "I have to say that sitting down with a complete stranger to watch a red patch slowly creep up your arm is not the most exciting. I sympathise with your affliction, but I was in the middle of working out a satisfyingly large invoice when she turned up, and that was a lot more fun."

What they couldn't know of course was that the half hour had been a big strain on me, too. The more I knew I was being watched, the more I felt I should do the five-times tapping. I had to keep concentrating on my feet in the hope that I'd be instructed to tap those, under the table, and that the visible bits of me would be left out of it.

"She was quite right, of course," said Mum. "If more people took action when they thought something was wrong ... But now I'm beginning to wonder if other people have thought the same thing and not said so. It's very unsettling. I can hardly go round accosting people and saying 'my child is not being ill-treated'."

"No one who's ever seen Dad would think he hit me," I said. "They'd know he hadn't got it in him."

But that didn't make them look any happier.

"Once you start knocking on doors," said Mum, "you never know what you're going to stir up. Think of that man at the corner, the one who tells Sarah to go home, you were obviously upset by what he said. Then the poor old woman in Park Street. She comes into the shop at least once a week and I spend hours trying to sort her out, one way or another, and I don't want to get drawn in as a neighbour as well. Enough's enough."

I'd forgotten I was worried about her, but that set me off again. "I never did get her watch right," I said. "I keep thinking I've made her miss her favourite radio pro-grammes."

"You never *can* get it right," said Mum. "She forgets to wind it, so even if someone helps her to get it spot on, the thing stops in about twelve hours and she's all at sea again."

"And that man," I said, "wants to stop them building because he wants to keep people out. I don't want to keep anyone out, I just want to save what's there. It's different."

"It comes to the same in the end," said Mum, and she got up and went into the middle room and switched on the TV news. "I'll start on the food in a minute," she said to the screen.

"There's nothing like a few national disasters to take your mind off the neighbours," said Dad, as he and I began to gather up the mugs and wash them. He mimed punching me in the eye to show he'd forgiven me. "Don't worry too much," he said, "all leaders have the odd dodgy follower. I just can't help wondering if it's worth all the anguish for six signatures." Then he went off to fetch Sam.

I thought we probably didn't need any signatures at all, now we knew we were a Conservation Area, but I didn't say so. I just addressed an envelope to the Planning Department at the Council Offices and begged a stamp. Having stirred up all those people it wouldn't have seemed right not to post the thing.

Next morning, though, the six signatures did look a bit feeble, so I left for school ten minutes early – not as easy as it may sound – and I knocked at four of the houses in our road that had been empty the day before.

The two girls next door were rushing out in opposite directions. They half listened to me, and they both signed, but I knew they only did it to shut me up so they wouldn't be late. Theirs was the garden Dad says is paved with good intentions. Actually, it's paved with concrete and has empty polystyrene urns blowing about in the breeze all over it.

Next door to them I disturbed the couple who have nothing out the back but the spreading magnolia tree. I obviously hadn't caught them at the best moment of their day. I could just see him through the far kitchen doorway, rasping at a piece of toast with a knife, in a cloud of black dust. She came and stood on the front step with a toothbrush in one hand and a dab of white on her chin. She didn't smile much, just foamed a bit at the mouth, but she did scrawl her name, leaving damp fingerprints all over the paper.

The next house was still empty, but at the corner the mother of the two little boys opened up and stood half glaring at me and half looking over her shoulder at some hand-to-hand combat that was going on just out of sight in the back room. "I can't stop," she said, before I'd finished, "or I'll never get us all out in one piece. You'll have to come back another time."

"I'm posting this now," I said, hoping the trees and crows and all were grateful for what I was doing. You have to care about something an awful lot to go out and annoy strangers, I find.

The two little boys were snarling like tiger cubs behind her, and I was sure she was going to slam the door on me, but then she said, "Give it here, then." She signed in the wrong place, in the margin, well away from the other names, and then she shoved it back at me and said, "And if I find you've conned me into sponsoring you for something, then I'm not paying, and that's that." Then she did slam the door, hard, and I could hear her shouting her way into the tiger's den.

Ten signatures would have to do, even if they didn't all come from the heart. I had a moment of panic as I wondered if the Council was likely to call on everyone who'd signed to ask them exactly why they objected. Then I remembered that we were Conserved, so they were unlikely to bother.

I rested the paper on top of the corner house gate and put down my own name, above all the rest. So what if I hadn't a vote, I thought, it was only a matter of time. My name came out a bit shaky, due to being written over a painted knothole in the wood, but there was nothing to be done about that, so I folded the petition, put it into its envelope, and set off for school at a trot, pausing only to push the envelope into a pillar-box on the way.

By the time Kathleen got back, Mum and Dad's paranoia was coming along nicely. Not surprising, I suppose. First it had turned out we had a history and a family – then one of them had moved in for a while – now neighbours were beginning to call, uninvited. The next stage, they were convinced, was that Kathleen was going to roll in from the cousins in the Midlands with an invitation for a family get-together.

When she did turn up, though, one Sunday afternoon, she didn't bring any messages from the present, just confusing stories of connections she'd made between English, Canadian and Australian cousins several generations ago.

A letter had come for her, from Canada, while she'd been away, and she was very pleased to get it. "It's from my husband," she said, and she took it up to the attic with her when she went to unpack her small case.

"That makes me feel awful," said Mum, when Kathleen was too far up the stairs to hear her. "I never thought to ask about her – I didn't even know she was married."

We knew when Kathleen reached her room all right because of the distant muffled thud. The rail didn't clatter so much, I'd noticed, when it fell down with clothes hanging on it.

"Pretend we haven't heard," said Dad.

They both made a big effort to be friendly to her when she came down again, but she didn't seem to want to talk about herself, she only wanted to talk about family trees. She'd cleared up some of the mysteries, she told us, that had made her put question marks on the family tree she'd sent us from Canada. "There was Benjamin Barclay, for example," she said, "son of Marion Bartlett's aunt, who seemed to have died two years before he was born. I'd checked his birth date and his death date, and they both seemed correct, and I couldn't work it out at all ..."

"Time warp!" said Sam hopefully.

But Kathleen said it was nothing so dramatic. "There were two Benjamins," she said. "One was a first son, who died in infancy, and when his parents had a second son, two years later, they called him Benjamin as well. People used to do that, it seems. Sad, really, as though one child could replace another. I'd found the death date of the first one and the birth date of the second one. Most confusing!"

"Anything about Marion Bartlett?" I said.

"A photo, that's all, so far," said Kathleen. "It's upstairs, I'll show you sometime. You know I said the people I was staying with are descended from her sister? Well, they gave it to me. They've also got a lot of family stuff unsorted in their attic. They wouldn't let me get at it, but they've promised to go through it while I'm still in the country. There just may be letters of hers – even a diary. I hardly dare hope!"

"I think she pushed me into taking the petition round," I said, to cheer her up. "So if she wants her letters found, I'm sure she'll push them to get on with it."

"I hope you don't really think," said Dad, when Kathleen had gone up to her room to sort her notes, "that you're being motivated from beyond the grave?"

"Don't worry, Dad," I said. "I expect you've got interesting ancestors, too."

"I think it's all very unhealthy," he grumbled. "The past is gone and should be left alone. All this is no more than primitive ancestor worship."

# Chapter Six

"You can be extraordinarily intolerant," said Mum sharply. "Just because you're not interested."

"Are you?"

"That isn't the point. It's history. Joanna could learn something."

I left them to argue over me without me, and went to tap on Kathleen's door. I wanted to have a look at Marion Bartlett. All the way up the stairs to Kathleen's attic I was thinking what I was going to say when I saw the picture. "That's amazing," I rehearsed. "She looks just like Mum – me – you," whichever seemed truest.

She didn't look like any of us, though, or else we didn't look like her, whichever way it goes. I took the small brown and white photo Kathleen passed to me and I saw a woman in a long skirt and a high-necked lace blouse standing in a faded garden. She was small and neat and upright, and she stared straight at the camera, but she didn't look particularly special.

"That was when she was back over here," said Kathleen. "Probably when she was living with her sister."

"Nice garden," I said.

"I'm sorry we don't have a picture of her in the North West Territories," said Kathleen. "I expect you find this a bit disappointing, a bit ordinary."

"I think I thought she'd look more intrepid," I said.

"Intrepid is as intrepid does," said Kathleen. "Knowing the kind of life she led and then looking at this and remembering when she lived, and the restraints there would have been on her, the restricting clothes, the fact that her father and then her husband would have had complete authority over her, makes her more impressive to me, not less."

Kathleen and I sat side by side on the bed, because we hadn't thought to give her a chair. I could see her typewriter standing on a suitcase on the floor, and I thought that she probably typed with the suitcase on her lap, like a desk. I thought I must remember to tell Mum we should provide something a bit better.

"When I said she was shoving me round with the petition," I said, "Dad thought I meant I heard spirit voices or something. I didn't mean that; I just meant I was thinking of her the way you do – thinking that if she could turn up at a strange lumberjack's camp on her own, then I could probably knock on a strange door in the next street."

"I keep remembering little bits and pieces my grandmother told me," said Kathleen, still looking at the photo in her hands. "One time, apparently, Marion Bartlett was in a missionary outpost, up a creek off the Mackenzie River. Winters are very long up there – the thaw may not come until June. This particular year they'd had exceptionally bad late spring weather – they were snowed in and supplies were running out.

"One afternoon they heard terrible noises – bangs like gunfire, and snapping noises as though huge trees were being broken up, and then earth-shaking grating sounds, as though the actual surface of the world was splitting apart. Someone climbed up on to the roof of the cabin for a better view and called down to the others that it was the thaw. It must in fact have been going on for a couple of days or more, it would take a while for the effects to be felt. Apparently great rafts of ice were breaking away from each other on the main river itself and also on the creek where they were. They were very excited.

"Most of them were new to the area so they didn't know how long it would take for everything to thaw. They were still trapped by snow, but all that day and all that night they heard the cracking, and the rasping sounds of ice floes scraping against each other as they began to move down river, and great thuds as lumps of snow fell off the few trees and off the roofs of their shacks.

"By next day they could actually hear the sound of running water from their creek, and also the roar of the river itself, still mixed up with the sounds of ice chunks crashing together. Then, just in time, just as they were feeling really happy and looking forward to being freed – they realised that the melting snows were raising the water level dangerously and that there were going to be floods.

"They took what possessions they could, on sleds, and they struggled away from the water to the higher ground. Everyone had to pull the sleds, harnessing themselves to them like huskies, but the flood waters were moving faster than they could, and they wouldn't have survived if a party of Caribou Indians hadn't come upon them and helped them along.

"The trouble was they'd built their shelter in a foolish place to start with, out of ignorance, but they just – just – got away with it.

"Of course, all this happened long before my grandmother was born, before Marion and Fred Bartlett had even met, but Marion had told her the stories and she'd remembered them and passed them on.

"That little figure in the Victorian lace blouse looks a lot more intrepid if you imagine it harnessed to a sled, struggling through melting snow, with flood waters hard on the heels of its boots."

"Yes, it does," I said, and I felt a bit guilty. "It's just that I find it hard to get to grips with things if I can't see pictures."

"I'm sorry," said Kathleen, "I haven't found any pictures, apart from that one." She looked as if she felt she'd failed again.

"Would you like to come through and see the garden?" I said. I knew it was risky. Showing someone something you care about a lot always is, because it's possible they may not see what's special about it. But I felt I had to do something in return for the Marion Bartlett story.

Kathleen looked a bit startled. "I'd like to," she said. "But are we allowed? Isn't it trespassing?"

I said there was nobody living there, so no one would know. Food smells were coming faintly up the stairs, onion mostly, and I knew Mum would call us to eat any minute. "We'll eat first," I said, thinking that would give Kathleen time to get used to the idea. "But we need to go straight afterwards. It gets dark about quarter past eight, I think."

We got off extra quickly because Mum wouldn't let Kathleen help with the dishes. She held up her hand when Kathleen started protesting, like a traffic policeman holding up a line of cars, and said, "I have my own routine."

"This is true," I said. "First she washes things in plain water, then she washes them in soapy water, then she washes them in plain water all over again."

"I simply rinse the worst off before I put the things in the bowl," said Mum, "otherwise the washing up water turns into soup before you're half way through. Disgusting! *And* I prefer to rinse the soap off and not eat it with my next meal, that's all. It's quite simple."

I said, "It takes forever."

"Now you see," said Mum to Kathleen, "why I find it easier to do it myself than listen to all the moaning and groaning."

We didn't say where we were going, and Mum didn't ask, but it must have been obvious and Kathleen looked embarrassed. "Come on," I said, "Marion made me take the petition round, now she wants to see what it was all about."

I'd forgotten that, though Kathleen wasn't at all fat, she was wider than me, and there was a bit of a struggle behind the hydrangea. Kathleen squeaked and the fence shook alarmingly, but we did get through, and I gave up the stump for her and sat on the ground.

The sun was low, so every blade of grass under the fruit trees, and every tiny roughness in their bark, had its own shadow. Every single leaf seemed as important as the whole garden. The glass roof of the conservatory looked as if it was on fire where the last rays were hitting it from behind. The saxifrage and aubretia were out now, blue, mauve and purple, and their colours seemed to get stronger as the light got dimmer. The chestnut tree was so thick with leaves that when small birds flew into it they disappeared completely. There was a terrific smell of garden – not flowers exactly, more a smell of green-ness and earthiness. There were pink flowers on the chestnut and the pigeons were crashing about among them, pulling at them, eating them I think, though they didn't seem to be doing much damage. I pointed out the pinky-brown one. "That one's new," I said, "joined the flock last week."

Both jays were flashing about, showing off, and almost as soon as we sat down a squirrel ran straight up the trunk of one of the silver birches. Its fur and tail were so silvery, in the evening sun, that you could almost believe it might be the spirit of the tree.

"Oh, this is so English!" said Kathleen.

"I should hope so," I said.

"But it's a perfect Victorian garden," said Kathleen. "Just the sort of place Marion would recognise from her middle years. Oh, look at the rook."

I explained it was Father Crow; he's easy to recognise because he's got a slightly droopy wing which you only notice when he's on the ground, walking away from you. "Just remember," I said, "if you see one rook, it's a crow, and if you see lots of crows, they're rooks." Then I suddenly remembered where Kathleen had just been. "I suppose this doesn't look much, after the country," I said.

"I've been in a welter of pesticides and herbicides," said Kathleen. "I think they call it the country. Any rooks or crows you see there are hanging upside-down by their feet."

"Any special reason?" I said.

"The farmers shoot them and hang them on a gibbet to scare off other crows. I've seen more wildlife here in three minutes than I saw there in three days, but I expect it depends which bit of the countryside you go to."

"They're used to us here," I said, "that's what it is. They trust us. They don't know people were planning to dump a million tons of concrete on top of them."

"Were planning?" said Kathleen. "Has something happened while I've been away?"

"This woman, Sarah," I said, "came round to sign my petition – well, really she came to see if Dad beat me up, but she signed while she was here – and she said her husband remembered when some people were trying to save a house about two blocks away they made it into a Conservation Area, and he says he's sure this block comes into the Conservation Area. So we're OK, I think. I still sent in the petition, even though it had toothpaste and things on it by then, because otherwise it would have been a waste of all that effort, but I don't think it was necessary."

"What's this about your father?" said Kathleen, putting her hand up to her cameo brooch. She had her dazed expression on again.

"That was nothing," I said. "Well, it wasn't nothing, really, I think he was a bit upset about it, but it all came right in the end. But it's good about the Conservation bit, isn't it?"

I got up because I wanted us to go in now. With two of us there, and with Kathleen being so much bigger than me, I was afraid we might be noticed by people from the other houses, and then they might all start to come in, which didn't seem like a good idea. I could imagine them picking flowers and hanging out washing and playing games and spoiling things. They could look at it, but I didn't want them messing about with it.

"Let me grasp the bits I understand," said Kathleen, and she stood up, too. "Is this man sure this is part of a Conservation Area?"

"He thinks it is," I said, "and it must be, mustn't it? If they were making one at all, they wouldn't leave out a garden like this, would they?" I went to the gap in the fence,

# Chapter Six

and I tapped the palings each side of it, discreetly, twenty-five times each.

Discreet or not, Kathleen noticed. "All right?" she said.

"Ants," I lied, and pretended to inspect the fence closely before going through.

"But what does 'Conservation Area' actually *mean*," said Kathleen, following me through onto our patch of grass. It was getting quite dark. I could see Mum had the light on in the middle room.

"It means," I said, "that everything in it is Conserved."

"I can see you think I'm being a bit stupid here," said Kathleen, standing on the grass and not going towards the house. "But think for a moment. If everything in this area is conserved, as you say, and has to be left as it is, why would the Council even consider a Planning Application for a lot of building? Surely they'd simply turn it down at once? They wouldn't write around to the neighbours, would they, there would be no point, no need."

There was still some lightness high in the sky, but down where we were darkness was beginning to seep up from the bottom of the garden walls. It gave me a weird feeling, as though the creeping darkness was somehow the same as the creeping doubts Kathleen was giving me.

"What do you think, then?" I said, not sure if I wanted to know.

"Let's work it out," said Kathleen. "There are several possibilities. One is that the man is mistaken, and it isn't a Conservation Area at all. Another is that it *is* a Conservation Area, but the Council have forgotten that it is, which doesn't seem very likely. Another is that it is a Conservation Area, but Conservation Area doesn't mean quite what you hope it does. Whatever, I think you should check it out."

Five blinks and five taps on the roof of my mouth with my tongue later, I said, "How?"

"Go down to the Council Offices. Ask."

"They wouldn't tell me."

"Of course they would. It won't be a secret."

"Marion Bartlett would go, I suppose."

"I think so. Come on, don't look so horrified. There won't be wolves or floods, I guarantee. I'd come too, but I've got to leave early tomorrow to get up to Edinburgh and check out the Scottish connections."

"I thought I'd done my bit," I said.

It's odd how you change. When Dad was saying no one would listen to me because I was too young to have a vote, I felt really cross about it. Now when Kathleen was saying that I ought to do more, I didn't like that, either. I thought, 'But I'm only a child, I can't be expected to cope with all this.' I didn't actually come out with anything so feeble, naturally. What I came out with was, "I'll think about it." No one could say *that* wasn't a grown-up answer.

# CHAPTER SEVEN

The Town Hall was unreasonably big, I thought, and very old and cold inside. It had a wide polished wood staircase, as well as lifts, and miles of corridors with rooms opening off them. It felt like a cross between a police station and a school; in fact it felt like the sort of place where you could get into big trouble for doing some little thing, like running or going through the wrong door. It just wasn't the kind of place where you would expect people to be nice to you.

I was out of breath and a bit dizzy when I arrived. I'd read the Council's letter again and seen that you could only go and look at the plans between nine and four on week-days. I didn't know how long it would take me to find my way to the right bit, once I was inside, and I was sure they'd throw me out dead on time – that's if they let me in in the first place – so I thought I'd better get there by half past three. School gets out at three, but the journey between school and the Town Hall is one of those you can't see how to do by bus. Buses go there, and buses go past the school, but none of them are the same bus, if you see what I mean. So I ran, all the way.

I was on my own, and I felt a bit pathetic about that, too. I'd thought Lynne or Sue might come along – they're quick enough to agree if I suggest going to the swimming baths or something. But whatever way I tried to describe what it was

I had to do, I couldn't seem to make it sound worth the effort, and they drifted off, swinging their plastic briefcases and giving me odd looks.

There was a Reception Desk in the Town Hall, and a woman there gave me directions to the Planning Department. She was one of those indignant grey-haired women who always look as though they're going to ask to check your fingernails – but whether she was indignant with me or just with life in general, I couldn't tell. The Planning Department was about as far away from the main entrance as it could be. I didn't enjoy going deeper and deeper into the building. I couldn't help wondering if I'd ever find my way out again.

The lift was all right, but then I had to walk down an empty corridor on a wooden floor with my footsteps sounding like hammer blows. I expected people to spring out of the rooms I passed, to see who was reconstructing their building, but no one did. Then there were double swing doors, and on the other side of those, there was a room with brown carpet tiles on the floor, and a big table, and a couple of plastic chairs and, at the end, a long counter. There was no one in there at all.

By this time, I didn't just have Marion Bartlett with me, I had the crows, the pine tree and a couple of squirrels as well. Although I really did know I was alone, I still felt I had to hold the swing doors open long enough for all of us to get through. It was as well there was no one else around – pine trees are very slow movers.

I went up to the counter and hung over it and looked both ways. I could see then that what had looked like a wall of the room was only a partition and that the space behind the counter went round it and into another room behind it, where I could hear voices. I didn't know if I was meant to knock on the partition, or what. I kicked around for a bit, sniffing and clearing my throat, and banging my plastic briefcase against the counter, but no one came.

# Chapter Seven

Then I saw the bell. It was one of those round bells that you're supposed to hit on the top with the palm of your hand. I still stood there, hoping someone would come without me having to ring it, but no one did and the clock behind the counter was saying twenty to four. So I stretched out my arm, shut my eyes, and smacked the bell, hard. The ping was surprisingly feeble but the voices behind the partition stopped. I held on to the edge of the counter and tried to imagine a timber wolf loping in behind it, so that whoever did come in wouldn't seem so bad. Who did come in was a man in a turban who didn't look too frightening and didn't seem particularly put out to see me.

"I don't know offhand if that's a Conservation Area," he said, when I'd explained. "I'll get someone to talk to you. Do you want to see the plans as well?"

"Is that all right?" I said. I kept thinking he was going to look round for my parents or someone, but he didn't, he just nodded and disappeared again. I could hear him opening drawers and talking to invisible men, and then he came back with a great roll of sheets of paper, and opened a flap in the counter and came out to my side.

"Come over here," he said, and he went to the table at the end of the room and put the roll on it. I don't know what I'd expected, but I certainly hadn't expected to see more than one plan. There seemed to be about a dozen, ink-drawn on crackly paper, all looking extremely important.

"Mr Penn will be with you shortly," said the man in the turban and he went off and left me to it.

I just looked at the great roll for a while and then I opened it out and began to try to separate all the different pages. It was awful. They wouldn't lie flat, they just bowled about on the table, bumping into each other, and even when I got one in a wrestler's grip and held it down on the table top with both my arms, I couldn't make much sense of it. Someone had drawn the block of flats they were wanting to put up where the house stood, and also all the houses they wanted to stick out in the garden, but they hadn't just drawn each of these things once – they'd drawn each one several times. 'Plan' it said on top of some of the pages. 'Elevation' it said on the top of others. It didn't say 'Conservation Area' anywhere.

I was determined to look at all of them, but they kept rolling about and curling up and I couldn't remember which I'd seen and which I hadn't, and somehow the 'side elevation' of the block of flats kept pushing itself forwards until I thought I'd scream if I unrolled it accidentally one more time.

I tried putting it to one side, and picking up something else from the pile that was left, but when I unrolled the one I'd just picked up its edge knocked the 'side elevation' onto the floor. I bent down to pick that up and the plan I had been looking at rolled itself up again with a snap and bounced gently to the left, knocking two more rolls onto the floor at the other side of the table.

"Don't *do* that," I said, and I picked them up and put them all on the table again and glared at them, trying to think of a plan for dealing with the plans.

"Having trouble?" said a voice, and I looked up and saw a youngish man coming through the flap in the counter. I thought he might be cross at the muddle I'd made of his crisp tubes of paper, but he didn't seem to be, just came over and got them under control for me. "The best thing," he said, "is to roll them all up inside each other, with the tops aligned, then you can look through for the one you want and take it out on its own."

I still felt he must think my parents were with me, really, on their way along the corridor perhaps, so I said, "I'm here on my own. I suppose I'm not meant to look at them as I don't have a vote."

"It's all the same to me," he said, bending down to put the big roll of plans on the floor under the table, keeping just one in his hand. "I'm permanent staff," he said, spreading the plan out, "I stay whatever happens in elections. Now, this is the overall plan. Hold that other corner, will you. Just lean on it – that's right. As long as you're serious and not messing about, I don't care how old you are or aren't."

"I haven't seen this one before," I said. "Each one I picked out seemed to be the block of flats."

"Yes," he said sadly, "they do that to you. It's very rare, you see, that anyone bothers to come and look at plans at all, that's why we're not equipped to display them flat."

The plan showed a crow's eye view of the whole block, but as it would be if the development happened. So the house and big garden were not there at all, and where the garage was, beside the house, the plan showed 'Access Road'. It took me a while to work out how it would look – then I spotted our house, and it became clearer.

"That's us," I said, pointing out the number. "They want to put a whole little town out the back of us."

"Hardly that," said Mr Penn. "But it's a substantial development, as they go."

"Can you tell me," I said. "Are we a Conservation Area?"

"Yes," he said. "As of about five years ago."

"Doesn't that mean you have to stop them doing all this?"

He looked at me. "Are you one of the objectors?" he said.

I was sure I must be on enemy territory, here, but luckily I'd got my right hand underneath the edge of the plan so I could tap out fives without him noticing. "I got up the petition," I said. It came out so apologetically that I was cross with myself. "I'm Joanna Watson," I said, more positively, "mine's the top name on the petition. You did get it?"

"We got it," he said. "We imagined you as much older."

"The others are," I said. "All the rest are grown up. All the rest have a vote."

"No need to be so defensive," he said. "I'm not prejudiced. It's just that your signature was rather shaky and we somehow pictured a little old lady in a lace blouse bustling about activating the neighbours."

Clearly they had expected Marion Bartlett. But I would have to do. "I signed on the top of a gate," I said.

"If you've seen enough," said Mr Penn, "we can stand back and let this thing curl itself up again."

When it had, he sat down on one of the plastic chairs and leant his arms on the table. "You see," he said, "Conservation Area doesn't necessarily mean all that much. Preservation Area is the one you need, if you want to stop all progress, but nothing in this area is deserving of such protection. To put it very briefly, Conservation Area means that you can't change the appearance of the front of your house, or cut down a tree in the front garden without permission. In a case like this, though, when all the development is to be out of sight from the main road anyway, permission would be unlikely to be withheld. It isn't going to change the area substantially, as long as the infrastructure can stand it, which it can." He looked up at me. I was still standing, holding on to the rolled plan with one hand to stop it bowling onto the floor. "Infrastructure," he said, "means drains and gas mains and so on. We wouldn't have allowed office buildings here, but I have to say that more housing in a residential area doesn't seem very significant."

I remembered my image of the great concrete foot, stamping out the secret heart of the block. "If you mean it's all OK because it won't show," I said, "What about the big house? That shows from the front."

He sighed. He did a lot of that, I noticed. "It's not a listed building," he said. "As far as I know, it's nothing special."

Suddenly, for the first time, it all seemed absolutely real. I'd imagined them destroying it rather the way, on a bad day, you might imagine yourself being run over by a bus, but somehow I hadn't ever thought that they really would do it. Now I could see someone had been out there, and measured, and then drawn pages and pages of plans, and brought them here and, for all I knew, filled in forms as well. I realised that no one was going to go to all that trouble unless they were very serious indeed.

"The garden, then," I said. "It's full of birds and there are squirrels and there must be mice or something because I've heard an owl hunting at night ..."

"Plenty of birds in London," said Mr Penn.

"So you're not going to stop them?" I said.

"Shouldn't think so," said Mr Penn.

If there was one thing I did not want to do it was to get tearful, but I had a sudden vision of old Father Crow waking up one morning to find nothing but cement mixers and bulldozers below him and trying to explain to Mother Crow what he was seeing. "Don't you care that we don't want all this?" I said.

He made a funny face before he answered, but it didn't really have anything to do with what I'd said, he was just trying not to yawn. It was very stuffy in the room.

"We always pay attention to objections," he said, "but – and I don't want to sound harsh here – but there really aren't many signatures on the petition, you know, and it really doesn't say much except that one or two people don't want change." He shrugged. "If you work in this department," he said, "you soon find out that no one ever does want change, but nevertheless it always happens, in some form or another."

Suddenly he stood up and unrolled the plan again. "Look at this," he said, "where did you say you lived? Here? Well there used to be a big house there, with a smaller one each side, mirror image of the one that's due for demolition. A bomb fell on the middle house in 1943 and destroyed it, and the damage each side was so great they pulled the lot down and built the terraces where people like you are very happy to live."

I said Dad had worked out that the reason the big garden was *so* big was that the owners of the house had bought extra land before the terraces were built.

"He's right," said Mr Penn. "And before the big houses themselves were built, the whole block was a market garden and orchard. I looked it up before I came out here. There's always change."

"There are apple and damson trees at the bottom of the big garden now," I said, hoping to get his interest. "About there, where those new houses go."

"Probably part of the original orchard," said Mr Penn, nodding. "And before that again, the whole area was fields, and the next block over was a copse. There would have been badgers and foxes and all sorts in those days. And I daresay if you dug down deep enough you might find fossilised dinosaur bones. Change, all the time change. It's part of life."

I said, "It's been getting worse and worse and worse. Can't we try and save some of what's left?"

He let go of the plan and watched it snap itself crossly into a roll again. "I'll tell you something," he said wearily, "in sixty or seventy years' time, when the new development is getting a bit tatty, and someone wants to pull it down and put up something else, there'll be people exactly like you getting up a petition to save that. And someone exactly like me will be considering the complaints. I guarantee it."

I said, "But you're not considering our complaints."

He sat down again and looked at me in surprise. "Oh I am. We are," he said. "It's just that they're not very convincing."

"So all those trees and things don't matter at all?"

"You mean the remains of the orchard?" he said. "If that's what those trees are, and it probably is, they must be very old by now. They'll be dying off naturally quite soon in any case."

It was obviously a mistake to talk about the orchard. I said, "What about the big trees, then. The pine and the chestnut, those ones?"

A flicker of interest did seem to come to his face then, so I told him about the poplar and the silver birches as well.

"I haven't seen the garden myself," he said, and he seemed to me to sound thoughtful. "And the developer hasn't submitted a detailed plan of what's there now. He's not bound to, of course."

"Couldn't you come and look at it?" I said, certain by then that something was just beginning to get through to him. "You could come to our house and look over the garden wall." I decided not to mention the gap in the fence in advance. "There's lots to see – there are all sorts of flowers as well, and little steps and things, and jays and crows and thrushes and the owl and the bats ..."

"Bats?" he said.

"I think they're bats," I said. "I saw them last summer."

He bent down and collected the rest of the plans from under the table and then rolled them inside the one that was still on the table top. "It's chucking-out time, I'm afraid," he said.

I'd been wrong. Nothing had got through to him after all.

I looked at the clock. It said ten past four. I couldn't think of anything else to say. I was terribly afraid that as soon as he'd got rid of me he'd forget everything, even the bits that had seemed to interest him – although 'interest' was probably too strong a word. Then he said, "I'll tell you what I'll do. This was coming up for consideration in a few days, but I'll get the date put back a bit and get someone along there to see what there is to see."

"Oh, that's great!" I said. "You can come into my bedroom."

He looked a bit startled and I could feel my face going pink. "I mean to look out of the window," I said. "It's got the best view of the garden."

"I think we'll get access to the garden itself, all right," he said.

He set off for the counter. As he raised the flap, I called

out, "You said there weren't enough names on the petition. How many should there have been?"

He hesitated. "The real problem," he said, "is that there aren't enough people in the whole block. But if you still want to try and make waves – individual letters are best."

"You should have had one," I said. "Dr MacGuire said she'd write."

He shook his head. "Just your petition," he said.

I thought of the people whose signatures I had managed to get. I couldn't imagine many of them writing a letter. Even the one I had thought was going to, hadn't, it seemed. "How important are the separate letters?" I said, hoping he'd say 'not very'.

"Hard to quantify," he said. "But ten separate letters definitely carry more weight than ten signatures on one letter. We all know that people sometimes sign petitions just because they're asked to. Feelings have to be running genuinely high to make someone sit down and put pen to paper."

"I'll try," I said.

"Good luck," he said, and he smiled a sad, sad smile – as if he somehow knew just exactly how much chance I had of succeeding.

# CHAPTER EIGHT

When Kathleen got back, with complicated stories from her latest trip, I listened politely before telling her my news.

You might think that two days of touring Scottish grave-yards would drag a person down, but she was all hyped up. Even the face on her brooch looked perkier. The big news was that she'd found the seventeenth-century gravestone of a couple who were half-Bartlett and half-Macdonald, and who she had always thought had died without having had children, and on this stone she'd managed to read the words 'beloved parents of Elizabeth'. This meant there was a whole other family line to follow up – or follow down, rather – because Elizabeth might have had children, who might have had children, who might have had children who might live in the next street for all we knew.

Kathleen said that discovering Elizabeth was just like hearing about a new birth in the family, but I somehow couldn't get excited about a three-hundred-year-old baby. I don't know if Kathleen was getting her own back on me, but she didn't seem to be able to work up much enthusiasm about my visit to the Town Hall, either.

Henry had jumped up onto her lap as soon as she sat down on the sofa, and she'd stroked his head all the time I was telling her what had happened. Then she just said, "If you want to achieve anything, you're going to have to be much more organised about things – you're going to have to work out a plan of action and carry it through."

I said, "I've got to do my homework."

I meant my homework from school, but she misunderstood me. "That's right," she said, "research is what's needed. Let's get to grips with this – what exactly is it you're trying to achieve?"

I thought that the latest invasion of ancestors must have pushed everything I'd told her out of her brain. "You know what I'm trying to achieve," I complained.

"Of course," said Kathleen, soothingly, "but you have to spell it out for me. It's good discipline."

Up to that point we three had been alone in the middle room, but just then Sam came wandering in to join us. It doesn't matter how far away Sam is, he can always tell if someone's giving me a hard time, and he doesn't like to miss it.

"I'm trying to save all that, out there," I said, "from the developers."

"The developers," said Sam, "are going to mash it all up and build over it." He lay down on the floor facing us, with his back to the TV, and began to play with the remote control. One of the programmes that kept flashing on and off behind his head was motor racing, and I suppose that gave him his next idea – "They might build a speedway track," he said, and began to add his personal sound effects.

"We *know* what they're building," I said crossly. "They're building flats and houses."

"Listen to yourself," said Kathleen, "you talk as if you're sure they're going to go ahead."

At that moment Mum called through from the kitchen, "it's very good of you to entertain Joanna, but do tell her to push off if you have things to do." I decided she probably couldn't hear what we were saying above the noise she was making with the blender.

Kathleen called back, "Not at all, I'm enjoying it."

## Chapter Eight

I thought it was nice to know one of us was.

"So tell me this," Kathleen said to me, "what is the point of trying to save something you believe is lost already?"

I said, "I thought you were on my side."

Kathleen said, "I am. Answer the question."

Right at the beginning I'd believed her when she said she felt nervous about going into strange libraries, but not any more. Right at that moment I thought that if anyone felt nervous it was probably the librarian.

I said, "I want us to go down fighting."

I thought that sounded rather good, sad and noble at the same time. Kathleen, though, was totally unimpressed. "Negative thinking," she said, sitting forward on the sofa. Henry jumped off her lap and strolled away. You're not supposed to move when you've got Henry, you're supposed to keep respectfully still, I would have thought anyone would know that.

"Now," said Kathleen, without attempting to apologise to Henry, "I agree with you that you're not going to win outright. No property developer is ever going to say, 'OK, we'll leave it all as it is and employ a gardener'. But you could win a few minor victories, and they just might be worth the effort."

"Like what?"

"That's what you have to decide," said Kathleen. "You have to decide if anything can be done, and if so what, and how to go about it."

Mum's voice came floating through from the kitchen again. "I know how demanding children can be," it said sympathetically. Even though she'd stopped using the blender she was obviously clattering around too much to hear what we were saying. Someone in the middle room was being demanding all right, but it wasn't one of the children.

"If you're going to get anywhere at all," said Kathleen, "you're going to need the support of as many of the neighbours as possible, and if you can't even convince yourself

93

that there's any point, then you're hardly likely to be able to convince them."

I was slouching in the corner of the sofa, feeling persecuted. Kathleen was sitting right on its edge, leaning a bit forwards, smiling encouragingly at me. Right at that moment it was quite obvious which of us was being inspired by Marion Bartlett. Then Sam's voice rose out of the chaos that was coming from the TV, saying, "Marion Bartlett'd crack it, I bet."

That gave me a really weird feeling, as if he'd known what I'd been thinking.

"What do you know about Marion Bartlett?" I said, far more fiercely than I meant to.

He half sat up, looking a bit surprised, and leaving the TV on the cartoon channel for the minute. "I know what you've told me," he said. "How she ran away to America – escaped from the Indians on the ice floe, all that."

I had told him the stories Kathleen had told me – I had thought he would enjoy them, and I'd been right – but I had told them exactly the way she had, I was sure of it. "She *never* went on an ice floe," I said. "The Indians *helped* them, they led them to higher ground when the river flooded."

"I like it best when she escaped on the ice floe," said Sam, and he rolled over onto his stomach and began to give serious attention to the cartoon, which the back of his head had obviously told him was worth watching.

Kathleen was talking to me again, but I couldn't concentrate at first. I couldn't have explained why, then, but what Sam had said had made me feel thoroughly unsettled.

" . . . so, from what you've told me of your Mr Penn's reactions," Kathleen was saying, "big trees are obviously a good point. You must check up on the Council, make sure someone does come along and look at them. I'm not sure how good the house is – probably not very – he certainly didn't sound impressed by it – but then you think he showed some interest in bats? Are you sure there really are bats?"

"I haven't seen any this year," I said, "but they were there last year. At least I think they were bats. Last year was a long time ago, and if you're going to stare at me like that and say, 'Are you sure?', then I don't feel sure at all."

"I have an idea, you see," said Kathleen, "that bats are a protected species. If so, they might be very good ammunition, as it were. I think you should find out."

"How?"

Kathleen glanced at her watch. When anyone looks at a watch I still feel depressed, thinking of old Mrs Potts and how time keeps getting away from her. "Isn't there a natural history museum, you could ask?" she said.

"They only have dead stuff!"

"They may know about live stuff as well. It's worth giving them a ring. Will they still be open?" She leaned over helpfully and showed me her watch. It was a quartz watch and I didn't think it went at all well with the old-fashioned brooch. I remembered Mrs Potts's pretty little old gold watch. "Unless you have any other ideas," said Kathleen.

I hadn't any others, I just didn't like that one. I hate talking to strange people on the telephone. Also, the telephone is in Dad's office, and I didn't want him to hear me making a fool of myself. Worst of all though, it had just come to me that I should tap the telephone one hundred and five times before making the call. One hundred and five! It had never got into three figures before. I decided they would finally lock me up when it got into the thousands. Then I tried to block off that thought in case thinking it made it happen. Even as things were, I couldn't believe Dad could possibly be so involved with his work in there that he wouldn't realise something peculiar was going on by the time I got to seventy-three or so. On the other hand, Kathleen was waiting for me to do something.

I looked away from her, to give myself time to think, into

the kitchen, past Mum, and out of the kitchen window. From where I sat I could just see the top of our hydrangea and of the fence, and the middle bits of two of the apple trees in the old orchard at the bottom of the big garden. As I looked, Father Crow made a very bad landing on an apple bough and almost immediately flopped off it again and out of sight. He's clumsy and heavy and little trees don't work for him, he needs big ones, with a bit of height and weight. If the big garden and everything in it went, there was nowhere in our little gardens that would suit him.

I mumbled about asking Dad to let me use the phone, and I went down the narrow hall to the front room office door, trying to do the hundred and five taps with my middle fingernail against the wall as I went. It slowed me up more than somewhat, but it gave me time to think, and by the time I'd got into Dad's office I'd decided to involve him in my problem.

Either things were going really well for him, or else he'd hit a very bad patch. Anyway, he was quite pleased to see me.

"Hello, work-substitute," he said.

He revolved himself on the stool in front of the drawing board while he listened to me, and then he said, "Are you still on about that garden? I'd have thought you'd have forgotten about it by now."

I explained about needing to be more organised and needing to have a plan of action, and he laughed. "Kathleen keeping you up to the mark, is she?" he said. "She's big on projects, that one."

Then he rang the Natural History Museum, while I sat on his huge desk and swung my feet a bit to make the point that I was a child and that it was only right that someone else should do things for me.

They told him bats are a protected species and they gave him another number, which he rang while I waited. "A bat specialist," he said to me across the mouthpiece while he waited for someone to answer. "Batman to the rescue!"

It was while he was talking to the bat-man that I began to feel really silly. Dad was doing his best, but he was getting it all wrong, and the bat-man was obviously asking him questions he couldn't answer properly. My feet and I grew up. I stopped swinging them, jumped off the desk on to them, and held out my hand. "I'll take it," I said.

Dad passed me the receiver with obvious relief.

I explained the position to the bat-man, and the bat-man explained the position to me. "Bats themselves are protected," he said, "and their roosts are protected, but their feeding grounds aren't. So if they're just feeding in the garden, there's not much anyone can do – but if they're actually roosting in the house, then the house can't be pulled down."

"Shall I go in and look?" I said.

"No," he said, "I'll do that if necessary. But keep watch, see if they are there. If you're quite sure they're around this year, and haven't moved away, get on to me again."

"Do I have to see them actually going into the house?"

"No. Just be sure they're in the area. If they're there at all, I'll come along, wherever they turn out to be roosting. But I've got a lot of other sites to look after and I don't want to come for nothing at all. ok?"

"OK" I said.

It was getting near eating time, so Dad came with me back into the middle room and he and Kathleen got into an incredibly boring conversation about American football. After all that, neither of them seemed particularly excited that I might have hit on something important. Sam was much better value, at first anyway.

"Lie," he said. "Say you've seen bats. I'll say I've seen bats."

"Can't," I said. "Can't bring that man all the way over here for nothing."

"I *have* seen bats," said Sam.

I looked him straight in the eye and he looked straight back.

"Truly?" I said.

"Truly," said Sam.

"This year?" I said.

"This week," said Sam.

"Describe them," I said.

"They come out after dark," said Sam, "and flitter about. And they have furry bodies and wings like leather." He held out his arms to demonstrate. "And mean little faces."

"You've seen them that close?" I said, wondering where I'd been while all this had been going on. "Wherever were you?"

"In this room," said Sam.

I looked through to the kitchen and out of the kitchen window. It was quite possible that Sam could have seen a bat flicking past the window, if one had chanced to fly through our garden just as he looked out, but even if he had binoculars, which he hadn't, I couldn't believe he would have been able to see its face.

"Sam!" I said. "This is important. You're not to lie to me."

"It's true," said Sam. "I saw lots of them. And I saw them roosting, all hanging up like umbrellas."

"Now I *know* you're lying," I said.

Sam drummed his feet on the floor in delight and smacked the TV screen with one hand. "It's true, though," he said. "I saw them on that."

"Then you are lying," I said. "You told me you saw them in the garden."

"Didn't!" said Sam. "I said I saw bats, from this room, and I did. You never asked if I saw them in the garden. You just thought I must have. See? I can say that to the developer and he'll believe me like you did, then he'll leave the house alone. Terrific, huh?"

I realised, not for the first time, that Sam didn't entirely grasp the problem.

The football conversation took us through into the kitchen to eat, and carried on right through supper, but afterwards Kathleen got back to me again, on a kind of summing-up note.

"I know this whole thing is your operation," she said, "and I don't want to interfere, but it's shaping up very nicely, isn't it?"

"How do you mean?" I said cautiously.

"Well, there are two obvious lines of action now," said Kathleen, "which is good. All you have to do is follow them and they'll lead on to the next move."

It was Sam's turn to take out all the rubbish, from every room not just the kitchen, and Dad was keeping him to it. Mum had got poor Henry in the garden and was waging chemical warfare against his first fleas of summer. I was alone with Kathleen, who was persisting in treating me like a grown-up.

"First," she said, after leaving a pause to see if I was going to come up with the plans myself, "you have to find out if there are bats – and second you have to persuade as many of the neighbours as possible to write their own letters. You did tell me that Mr Penn said that could help?"

I had told her. I had only myself to blame.

"If you knew the trouble I had with that petition," I said plaintively.

"Leaflet them," said Kathleen.

"What?"

"If you go and stand on the doorstep and badger them," said Kathleen, "most of them won't really listen to you, they'll be too busy thinking how to get rid of you. People are like that, they hate to be hassled. But if you do a really good leaflet – just a short one, on your father's word processor, and put one through each door, each person can read it at his or her leisure and then some of them might act on it."

"What – you mean just something saying 'please write'?"

"It needs a bit more than that," said Kathleen. She ticked off points on her fingers. "One, you have to tell them why separate letters are important. Two, you have to tell them there really is a chance of some kind of success. Three, you have to give them some points to make in their letters, in case they can't think what to say. Tip them off that big trees and bats seem to carry some weight, as it were."

Henry scooted through the room at high speed and fled down the corridor and up the stairs. He left a faint sickly smell of flea spray behind him.

"I have homework," I said. Hours seemed to have passed since I'd last said that, and still I hadn't done any of it.

"Oh, well, I'm not advocating skipping homework," said Kathleen calmly, and she dropped the subject.

I went up to my room. Henry was trying to get under the bottom bunk but there wasn't room for him what with all the junk from Kathleen's attic. He saw me and crouched flat on the floor, ready to run. It's the only time he loses his dignity, when he's been sprayed. It's very understandable. I wouldn't want to smell like that either. I talked to him for a bit without going near him and he understood that I wasn't about to give him a second going-over. He relaxed a bit and got on to the bottom bunk and began to wash. Every now and then he broke off and licked the air and then sneezed. It must taste filthy, that stuff, I'm sure he'd prefer the fleas.

I got my books out of my plastic briefcase and I sat down at my desk in the window. It was still light, but the sun was getting low. The crows were all in their tree, though not in their nest. The two young ones were nearly as big as their glossy parents now.

One of the magpies came and stood for a second on our end fence, in the full low sun, and I could see clearly that the parts you think are black are really a vivid dark blue-ish, green-ish colour.

A squirrel was sitting bolt upright in the middle of the

right hand bit of lawn, just in front of the conifer. It wasn't looking much like a lawn now, I noticed, the grass was very long and there were daisies. I'd never seen daisies there before. The squirrel, though, was sitting just tall enough for me to see it above the grass. It was washing its face.

The blackbirds were making their usual evening fuss in the shrubbery. They always give a regular metallic-sounding shriek in the evenings, a kind of urgent scolding. It's a bit unsettling. I used to think they were warning that night was coming. Now I began to wonder if they somehow sensed other danger.

I got up again and I went downstairs and Dad said, yes, I could use the word processor, he'd knocked off for the evening anyway, and I sat in the front room office for two hours until I thought I'd got the leaflet right.

Night really had come by the time I went back upstairs again. No one had asked about my homework so no one knew I had to sit up till twelve to do it. I began to understand why Dad gets ratty when he's interrupted and he has to work late to finish up.

I kept my curtains drawn tightly across my window while I sat at my desk, and I left them that way when I fell into bed, which was unusual for me. I could hear the owl occasionally, but I wasn't ready to look for bats yet. It wasn't anything to do with not liking bats – I like bats a lot. I just felt too tired to face the disapppointment if they turned out not to be there after all.

# CHAPTER NINE

Staying up till midnight isn't too bad at the time, but it definitely turns the next day into an uphill struggle. I didn't actually go to sleep in class, but I wasn't what you could call alert, either. I found I could pay attention to the first halves of people's sentences, but I somehow couldn't be bothered to listen to the last bit, and I was surprised how quickly I lost the thread of what was going on. This didn't go unnoticed, and I was feeling severely got–at by the time I reached home.

It was sunny and very warm and I began to fantasise about taking a rug through the gap in the fence, putting it down under an apple tree and going to sleep on it. I'd never done that before, but it sounded like a nice way to spend an hour. Henry could join me. If anyone in the house lies down in the daytime, Henry always appears and flops down beside them. I think he feels that lying down is one of the few sensible things we do.

I went to dump my briefcase in my room. There on my desk was the neat pile of leaflets I'd printed out, and I guessed that at some point during the evening Marion Bartlett would turn up, disguised as Kathleen, and want to know whether or not I'd delivered them.

I was getting a bit sick of Marion Bartlett. She seemed to me to have set rather high standards for the rest of us, and I didn't think it was really fair. For all any of us knew, I might turn out to be extremely brave myself if a river near me flooded. And for all any of us knew, Marion Bartlett might have been really weedy about her neighbours. In fact, she might have gone off to the snowy wastes on purpose because she was better at dealing with bad weather than awkward people.

I sat at my desk for a bit, thinking of all the people in the world who are probably incredibly heroic but no one ever knows about it because nothing ever happens in their lives for them to be heroic about.

Then I began to wonder what would happen to you if you were a gifted pianist who had been born before pianos were invented, or a potential Olympic swimmer who lived all your life in the Sahara Desert.

And then I felt really depressed.

I got up and hung out of my bedroom window. The garden was looking really lush. The trees were heavy with green, you could just see the tiny beginnings of fruit in the orchard, the herbaceous border had shot up high and there were foxgloves in it now, which I'd never seen there before. I realised how much pruning and cutting and trimming and weeding old Mr and Mrs Owner must have done in their day to keep it all in shape. That was what was beginning to go – the shape. I could no longer quite see where flower beds ended and long grass began. A pair of white butterflies went dancing about beyond the apple trees, showing up well as they passed one of the dark conifers.

It had been beautiful before but in a way it was better now, more relaxed, much nicer for the birds and all the other things that lived in it. But not for long. Just as everything was really beginning to enjoy itself and multiply, a whacking great block of flats and several large houses would land on top of it, wiping it out forever.

Unless, of course, I posted lots of bits of paper with words on them through the local letter-boxes. Put like that,

I seemed about as likely to achieve anything as Dad had always said I was – or wasn't.

The two little boys were out in their garden, kicking a ball around as best they could, somewhat limited in their movements by the big blue climbing frame. It must have seemed like such a good idea when their mother bought it.

The Fusspots were outside, too, picking about at their roses and muttering to each other. It was all very well, I thought, for them to refuse to sign anything unless my parents signed first, but how were they going to feel when there was a building site just over their back wall. Often when Sam is yelling around in our garden those two grey heads appear above the fence as a protest. The fence between them and us is quite tall, and they're not, so they must stand on something, side by side, to send over a double dose of disapproval. Sam's voice can definitely hit some very disturbing notes at times, but never anything to compare with a demolition gang and a cement mixer. I planned an unflattering diary entry about them.

Sarah was out in her garden, way over on the other side, holding her baby as usual, but she was standing with her back to me, talking to the children in the garden beyond hers.

And Mr Dahlias was out, too, behaving rather oddly, I thought. He wasn't admiring his flowers, he was leaning on his end wall with his elbows, looking through a pair of binoculars at the big house. I couldn't make out what he was watching – the butterflies, maybe. The birds were mostly out of sight – they do seem to vanish for a while in the afternoons – except for the pigeons, who were sitting on the house roof in their usual way.

Suddenly, something appeared over to my left, on the end wall of the doctors' house. A little slinky black cat. It dropped down almost at once into the big garden and out of sight. I'd never seen that before, that was new – I couldn't imagine what Henry would think about it.

## Chapter Nine

Then I saw that all the polystyrene urns in the garden on our other side had been stacked up and a barbecue had appeared. It wasn't lit or anything, the two girls wouldn't be home from work yet, but the sight of it made me feel hungry and I went down to find a snack before going out on my delivery round. Sam had had the same idea, and by the time Mum came home, and Dad wandered through, we'd got a couple of good sandwiches together – banana and cream cheese in mine and peanut butter and raspberry jam in his.

"Blood of the vampire," said Sam, licking off a trail of jam that was sludging its way up his arm. "What if those bats out there are vampires?"

"You don't get vampire bats in this country," said Mum.

"You do in zoos, I suppose," said Dad.

"Escaped vampires," said Sam. "We could catch them and train them to attack the Developer."

"They probably wouldn't attack one of their own kind," said Dad.

"The Developer," said Sam, "will be having razor blades in his sandwiches, razor blades and ground up light bulbs."

"You see what happens if you're not careful what you say," said Mum to Dad. "The child's got a full blown prejudice against someone he knows nothing about. No developer has ever done him any harm."

"Not yet," said Dad.

"Very funny," said Mum, not laughing at all. "How do you expect the child to know you're joking."

Whenever Mum refers to either of us as 'the child', I feel as if I ought to be somewhere else. It usually means it's a private argument and we're not meant to join in.

I went out and left them to it.

Letter-boxes are extremely variable. I'd never realised that before, because ours is very ordinary – it's in the middle of the door and it's easy to push open from the outside. But once I got going round the block I found upright high-up ones, and low down ones right at the bottoms of their doors, so I had to get on my hands and knees to push my leaflet through. I do not wish to be a post-woman when I grow up. The bird lady's letter-box had a horrible whiskery fringe behind it that groped at my hand as I pushed the thing through, and the man with the dahlias and the eyebrows had such a vicious spring on his that it bit my knuckles. The note he ended up with was scrunched into a ball and probably had dabs of blood on it.

The second to worst was the house next to the bird lady. The flap gave easily enough, and I pushed my hand right through, but just as I was about to let go of the leaflet I felt a sort of warm wetness and realised I was pushing it right down the throat of the dog the other side. I suppose it must have opened its mouth to bark and been leafletted before it could make a sound. I got my hand out fast. I don't like to think what happened to the leaflet. What made it worse was that I'd never seen the dog out in its back garden so I didn't even know what sort it was. Sam would have said it wasn't a dog at all. He'd probably have decided it was a werewolf. I wiped the dribble off on my skirt and hoped that, as it hadn't actually bitten me, I wouldn't get rabies or anything.

The absolute worst, though, was Mrs Potts's house. I saw her eye at the curtain hole as I went up the path, and I tried to push the thing through the door and get going fast, but she's surprisingly nippy on her feet and before I was out of her gate she was at the door calling to me. Her watch had stopped, she said, and she was afraid she'd miss *The Archers*.

This time I understood the problem a bit better, so I started off by giving her the correct time plus two minutes, and I just kept on saying the same time when she asked, no matter how long she fiddled on. In the end we got it set just two minutes slow, which was the best I could manage. Better than it not going at all, I felt.

But it got to me. I don't know why, it really got to me, the thought of her all alone in that house in her pink feathery

slippers, with all her favourite radio programmes starting
without her just because I'd taken the easy way out. I fretted
about it all the rest of the way round the block and then, just
as I got back to our door, I had the brainwave. I looked at
my own watch. It wasn't even five yet. He should still be
there, the man I had in mind.

I didn't go indoors. I went straight on for several blocks
until I got to the turning that leads to the High Street.
There's a big double-fronted shop in the High Street, empty,
with whitewash all over its windows and workmen crashing
around inside. He's usually standing in the doorway, with
his suitcase propped open, and he's often there till after the
real shops have shut – I suppose he does a bit of trade with
people going home from work. So although I ran or jogged
most of the way, it wasn't so much because I thought he
might have gone, it was because I was so excited by my idea
that I wanted to carry it out straightaway, at once, immediately.

There he was, standing in the sun in his open-necked shirt
with rows and rows of watches in his huge flat suitcase.
They come in all sorts of colours and patterns and things,
but they are all incredibly cheap – and they are all quartz.
You don't have to wind them. They just go. They just go on
and on until one day they don't go any more. But until they
stop forever, they tell you the right time, even if you're Mrs
Potts who can't remember about winding things.

I couldn't imagine why no one else had ever thought of
this obvious answer before.

I chose her the plainest I could find. It had a transparent
strap and a grey face, and it had numbers around the face.
Most of them either have dots or nothing at all, and I felt she
might not be up to telling the time without numbers.

It seemed an unbelievably long way back to her house. I
kept trying to work out what she'd say. Either she'd be very
pleased, quite touched even, or else she'd think I was inter-
fering in her life and come on all ferocious. I was really

nervous and out of breath by the time I rang her doorbell.

Well. She was pleased. She was delighted. It couldn't have worked better – at first. I explained it to her, about it being quartz and what that meant, and her eyes went all watery and she said that nobody else had cared about her missing her programmes, and she didn't mind what people said about the young of today, there were those of us who had hearts of gold. We were both quite overcome by the time I was turning to go away down the path again.

And then – she held the watch firmly in her left hand, grasped the tiny knob between the finger and thumb of her right hand, and said to me, "And *this* time, dear, I promise I won't forget to wind it." And she turned the knob, to demonstrate, turned it and turned it, spinning the hands around the face, on to New York time, Hong Kong time, Sri Lankan time, who knows what time – certainly not South London time.

I went home. There are things you can do and things you can't do, Dad says, and I think Mrs Potts was a bit out of my range.

# CHAPTER TEN

Then I went on bat watch. I had to wait till just before dusk which, now that summer was really getting going, was a bit later than I'd realised. I said I was going up to start my homework, and I did my secret creep out into the garden. I did it in a very half-hearted way, but it worked well enough. I really didn't want Sam with me. I knew I wasn't exactly far from home, but there are times when you don't need to hear vampire stories and this was one of them.

I sat on the stump as the light faded and I watched the moon begin to rise behind the chestnut tree. The blackbirds had scolded themselves to sleep, and the high crows' nest looked empty, but I guessed they were at home, lying low. It was very quiet and secret out there, with not much moving at all, except a column of midges rising like smoke out of the top of the pine.

It wasn't truly dark because of the moon. I could see everything, but the colours had gone dim and merged together, and in some places two trees had melted into one so that the whole place looked a little bit different, a little bit strange, sort of liquid.

I thought I saw a movement in one of the top windows of the big house, but I wasn't looking directly at it when it happened, and when I did look it wasn't there any more, so I couldn't be sure.

I sat right in the middle of my stump, holding on to its sides with both hands and tapping five times with each finger in turn against the bark; to make the bats come, to keep me safe, I didn't know.

All right, Marion Bartlett, I thought, you'd better take over now, this is your kind of thing, the great outdoors. Then I decided she'd be very scornful of my venture. A bat stake-out in the next door garden hardly competes with being swept down river on an ice floe.

Kathleen hadn't come back at the end of the day after all. She'd taken herself off on one of her ancestor-hunting trips while I'd been at school. She hadn't announced what she was going to do, she'd just vanished, leaving a note leaning on the kettle to prevent anyone including her when they planned the next meal. I think she meant to cause the least possible disturbance by doing it that way, but I found it very unsettling.

The column of midges appeared to me to be just a bit closer, though it was still very high up. I blinked at it five times, to keep it at bay.

Marion Bartlett on an ice floe! Marion Bartlett had never been on an ice floe, that had been an invention of Sam's, and he'd got me at it now. I remembered I'd felt uneasy when he'd first come out with all that. If Sam could make something up and pass it on to me, how did I know that other people, in the past, hadn't done exactly the same thing? The stories about Marion Bartlett had been handed down from her daughters, Kathleen had said. But her daughters hadn't been born till after she'd done all these intrepid things of hers. Maybe she really did go out to the North West Territories on her own, but maybe her trip was rather uneventful and maybe, just maybe, her daughters added the floods and the Indians to spice it up a bit. It was possible.

I sat there sniffing the air like Henry does. The honeysuckle was out and the pink roses on the ancient bush hanging over the pergola were in bud, and their scents were blending with the rich smell of leaves and grass, and the fainter breaths from the fat bunches of aubretia and from the herbaceous border.

I was beginning to want to be a bit more sure about Marion Bartlett, but I felt I couldn't really ask Kathleen because it might look as though I was trying to take away her prop. And I did understand about people needing props – one, two, three, four, five; one, two, three, four, five.

Then I really saw a movement – in one of the downstairs windows of the big house. There couldn't have been anybody there really, I thought, because it was all locked up. I wondered if something had moved past the outside of the window and made a reflection in it. Perhaps even a bat. Maybe a bat had flitted by without me noticing and my eye had just caught the movement of its reflection in the glass. It had looked bigger than a bat, though.

I glanced round. From where I was sitting I could just see parts of the top windows of some of the surrounding houses. They were all in darkness, but a glow in the hedge on the far right, and a dimmer glow coming through on the left, showed that some people had their downstairs lights on. It's always darker inside than out, and there was no light showing behind any of the windows of the big house. I was sure no one could see to move around in there without one. Unless of course it was a ghost.

I began a short fantasy where it turned out that it's possible for people who are still alive to haunt places. In this fantasy, what I had seen was one of the living ghosts of Mr or Mrs Owner. It would turn out that wherever they were now, they were missing their old home, so their 'other selves' were still wandering around in it. I, of course, would make this discovery, and I would write a paper on it, which would be published, and which would take the scientific world by storm. However, I abandoned the fantasy early on because it was rather disturbing. I don't want to see people who aren't really there, even if they are alive and well somewhere else.

The column of midges was definitely a little closer. It was half way between the pine and me, and much lower down. I decided that when the first scout broke free and bit me, I'd go indoors. Let's face it, Marion Bartlett, that's about what you'd expect from someone who conducts a safari within shouting distance of her own back door. To be fair to me, the midge column was quite threatening. It was shaped like a tornado and it looked like something that was mainly still but at the same time was waving about a bit in the breeze. There wasn't a breeze, though, and when I looked more carefully I could see that every individual midge in the column was spinning about, up and down and sideways, but never far enough sideways to spoil the shape of the column.

A little moth, very small and discreet, passed me by and went to sit on one of the half-opened buds of the honeysuckle which was draped over the shed. Then something awful flew by, a kind of large insect with far too many legs. I didn't look closely. There were no bats.

I sat there very still, very silent, and I thought that if there was all this bat food about and no bats it could only mean one thing – that they'd moved out last year.

A swallow went by, high above. It was almost dark in the garden now, but the sky was still light, and I could see it dipping past, going home disgracefully late.

As I looked down from the sky, I saw another movement, in the conservatory beside the big house, a real movement, not my imagination. What it was, though, was the movement of someone going from the conservatory through the door that joins it to the house, so by the time I'd seen it, it had already gone.

Vandals, squatters, ought I to tell someone?

Just as I was wondering, a dim light came on in the downstairs room of the house, behind the french windows, a dim light that moved about. For a second I thought someone was setting fire to something, but it was a steady light, and I realised it came from a torch. Half a second later, before there was time to think what that might mean, the french windows opened and a dark figure stood there, aiming the torch into the garden. This torch had a powerful beam and whoever was holding it swung it right around the garden in an arc, like the beam of a small searchlight.

Then two things happened at exactly the same time. One was that the beam of light hit me directly in the eyes as it went by, which I knew meant that whoever was behind it had probably seen me, and the other was that a shape blipped through the beam. It might seem unlikely that I would recognise something that I saw for only a millisecond – and just before I was dazzled by torchlight – but there are a few shapes that could only ever belong to one thing. A bat shape cannot possibly belong to anything but a bat.

I half got up, crouching, to go back through the fence at speed, but as I did the torch beam came back and landed right on me, and a man's voice called out, "Just a minute. What are you doing there?"

He was already walking at speed down the garden towards me, but it's a long garden and I could have got through the fence before he reached me. The reason I didn't was that his voice sounded official, like a school teacher, and I thought I knew who he was – I thought he was the beat policeman keeping an eye on tne house, and I thought that if I stood my ground and explained that I wasn't doing any harm it would be better than if I ran and was chased into my own house by the law. Sam'd have loved it, but Mum and Dad might not have been so keen.

I did get my back right up against the fence, though, with one arm already through the gap, just in case. And I blinked in fives, and I tapped my tongue in my mouth in fives, and I scratched at the fence in fives. I wouldn't want to pretend I was brave, or anything.

He wasn't wearing police uniform, he was wearing an

ordinary suit, and as he came through the orchard at me I could see he was very tall. I got my shoulder through the gap as well as my arm, and one foot. He didn't shine the torch right on me again, he shone it on the ground between us, and what with that, and the fact that the sky still wasn't totally black, and the bit of half moon that was gleaming above the chestnut, I could see him quite well. I had to look right up to see his face, though, and as I did I kept noticing a black flittering thing passing across the sky behind his head. It gave me a funny feeling. I do like bats, and I was very pleased they were still there, but somehow you don't want them around when you're faced with a very tall, strange man who has suddenly appeared out of an empty house in the dark. Just prejudice, I guess.

"You realise you're trespassing?" he said.

I whined something about not doing any harm, and thought how bodies always, unfailingly, let you down. My voice sounded the way it had when I was six-years-old and in trouble, and my top lip was prickling, obviously planning to develop a blob.

"You may not be doing any harm," he said, "but you shouldn't be in here at all. This garden is private property, my property."

I was alone in the garden, in the dark, with the midges, the bats and the Property Developer. I couldn't wait to tell Sam.

Marion Bartlett came hurtling to my rescue. "How do I know *you're* not trespassing," she said, in my normal voice, "creeping about the house with a torch."

"I need a torch because the power's turned off," he said. "I came to check the old fireplaces – we'll take them out first. It gets dark earlier than I'd remembered. That's my story – what's yours?"

It didn't seem a good idea to mention the bats just then, so I said, "I come in to watch the birds. I don't go near the house."

# Chapter Ten

"The birds!" he said. He had quite a loud voice. "It's a bit dark for birds!"

"There's an owl," I said. "I just live through there and I never come in further than that stump so it can't possibly count as trespass. I'm almost in my own garden, really."

"Then I think you'd better get *right* into your own garden," he said, "really, really."

There was nothing I wanted to do more. There was the garden, all liquid in the dark so that it could, if it wanted, turn into something quite else – and there was this shadowy figure who'd somehow become part of it, so that it seemed possible for him to become something quite else, too.

Then he said, "Before you go, do you know most of the people round here?"

"Some," I said.

"Do you know where someone called Joanna Watson lives?" said the looming Property Developer, while bats flew round his head and the midges closed in. My knees gave way a little bit, but enough of me was half through the fence for the boards to support me. For some reason, Marion Bartlett gathered up her skirts and stomped off. "Why?" I squeaked.

"Because," said the Property Developer, "she's causing me a lot of trouble and I'd like to have a word with her and find out why. I want to put up a nice little development in here, and for some reason the neighbours are trying to throw a spanner in the works. I've seen a petition at the Planning Department with Joanna Watson's name at the top. I understand she's co-ordinating it all."

The edge of the fence gap was digging into my shoulder and also into my ankle. I found it very reassuring.

"I'm Joanna Watson," I said.

He glared down at me. He was older than Dad, but not really old, and from what I could see of his suit it was a lot slicker than anything Dad ever wears.

"YOU are?" he said. "You mean YOU'RE stirring up all these people?"

Then he stared over my head as if he'd lost interest in me, but at the same time I could tell he was crosser, and I understood why, because I was beginning to feel cross too. Nice Mr Penn, who had said that if people were interested he was glad to help, even if they were too young to vote, was having a good laugh at both of us. He must have deliberately pointed out my name at the top of the petition, knowing that we just might meet, and knowing that the Developer would feel silly when he saw me. Well that was OK, but what about me? I suddenly understood why Sam hates being got-at for being short. I'm the right height for my age, but I was a lot less than the right height for the Developer, and I didn't like it at all.

My top lip was beginning to feel warm as well as prickly, and when I touched it with my tongue I could tell it was sticking out, just a tiny bit, over the bottom one.

"What on earth are you doing this for?" said the Developer. "Is it a joke, or what?"

"No," I said. "We all – everyone round here – we all love this garden and we don't want it spoilt. You think no one knows what goes on in the middle here, because it's hidden, but we do know, we see it all the time."

I've never been the sort to answer back in class and I was quite impressed. But he just looked at me, and then he said, "Don't you think you should be ashamed of yourself?"

I touched my top lip with my tongue five times – my problems seemed to be meeting each other – and then I said, "Why?"

"Because," he said, "you're a very selfish little girl, wanting to keep a garden that isn't even yours, when the space could be used to build homes for lots of people."

I thought that if my allergy was any use it would start up all over me, not just on my lip, so that I would swell up like a bullfrog and he wouldn't be able to call me 'little girl' any more. Then I thought that it might yet do just that – I hadn't eaten any chocolate, so the only logical conclusion was that I really was allergic to developers.

"It isn't only the garden itself," I said. "We want to save it for the wildlife."

"Wildlife!" said the Developer, and he flashed the torch quickly around, shining the beam at the bottoms of bushes – but nothing moved, not even a hedgehog. He was entirely unaware of the overhead bats. "You don't get wildlife in South London, darling, you get wildlife in Africa, and most of that's in game parks."

A far distant bat flickered at the edge of the house roof and then disappeared. That must be where the roost was, I thought, it really must, but I still didn't draw his attention to them. I felt it might not be wise until someone official had seen. But I said, "There are squirrels, and there must be mice or something because there's an owl, and there are lots of different birds."

"Birds, my darling," said the Developer, "will go somewhere else. They'll fly there. That is why they are equipped with wings. And squirrels are just a menace – they're rats – destructive tree rats."

I put the chewed cable out of my mind. "We like them," I said, "and there are all kinds of other things – butterflies and blackbirds and magpies and all sorts."

I didn't mention the crows. I would have felt I was giving them away to the enemy, while they snored in their high nest, with no idea of what was going on.

The Developer flung his arms up in an impatient gesture, and the torch beam search-lighted across the sky. "It's all a lot of hypocrisy," he said. "It's only the furry, pretty things you care about. If birds and squirrels were bald, and if the principal creatures in this garden were spiders and cockroaches and puff adders, you'd be begging me to develop, as quickly as possible, and get rid of the lot."

I was sure there was a flaw in his argument, but I couldn't spot it in time. I just stood there, blinking five times and clenching each foot inside its shoe five times.

He stopped sounding angry and sarcastic and put on a kinder voice. "You *must* realise," he said, "that people are more important than birds."

I thought that needed some thinking about as well, so I still didn't say anything.

That made him snappish again. I wasn't surprised, the kinder voice hadn't suited him at all. "I'm going to go ahead and develop here anyway," he said, "whether it suits you or not, so you're simply wasting everyone's time. The Council is unlikely to be concerned about the objections of someone who doesn't even have a vote, anyway."

"I will have one some day," I said, twitching most of my moveable parts in fives, "and my parents vote." I hurried on in case he asked what they thought about it all. "And anyway, the neighbours agree with me." Some of them did – I hadn't said all.

"The neighbours!" he said, "How many of them are there? Forty or fifty at most. Let me tell you, when there were objections to the road widening scheme at the top of the High Street, do you know how many signatures were on the opposing petition? Three thousand! And the scheme went ahead anyway. You can't possibly win, all you can do is cause a lot of bother and hold things up for a few months, and cost me a lot of money."

"That'll have to do, then," I said, and I stared straight back at him. He tried to look me fiercely in the eye, but he kept glancing down at my lip. I knew by the feel of it what it must look like by then, a great glossy bolster. It seemed to fascinate him, which was understandable.

Then he smacked the back of his neck hard, looked at his hand, and wiped it briefly on his trousers. "Midges," he said. "No point standing around here, being eaten alive – I think they've already bitten you. Just remember, will you, that I'm not impressed by silly behaviour. Now, it's time you went. You'd better come back out through the house with me."

"No," I said, inching a bit further through the fence. "I go through here."

To my horror, he reached out and caught me by the elbow. "That's the trespasser's route," he said. "You'll go out the proper way."

I didn't pull back, he was obviously stronger than me. I let my arm go completely limp until I felt him relax his grip. Then I snatched it free and reversed through the fence.

He didn't try to grab me again, just said, "Well see you don't do any damage."

Damage! Me! I stared at him in amazement through the gap.

"Remember," he said, "that this is my property and in future I shall take a very firm stand indeed on trespassing." Then he turned his back and strode off through the dark garden, flicking the torchlight to and fro ahead of him with one hand, and flapping at the midges with the other.

I turned to face home – and I found I felt quite peculiar – a bit unreal.

There was a glow coming from the attic and the bathroom windows, but the bottom of our house was black-dark, which was unusual, and I could only just make out the shape of Henry, sitting upright on the side fence and staring down towards the ground. At first I couldn't see what it was he was looking at, but I could hear a strange muffled croaking noise coming from somewhere below the kitchen window.

I took a step forwards and Henry made as if to jump down from the fence to greet me, then he changed his mind and stayed where he was, still staring down, as if there was something below him that he didn't want to meet at close quarters. From the angle of his head I knew that whatever it was he was worried about was between me and the back door, so I stood still for a moment while my eyes got used to managing without the Developer's torchlight. I looked towards the sound, a kind of eerie low moaning, not like anything I'd ever heard before. The liquid unreality seemed to have flooded right through into our dark little patch.

Then I saw it. It was a small winged goblin, writhing and complaining on the ground.

As I looked, it let out a great harsh scream, arched its back, and seemed to split in half.

For one horrible, mad moment I thought it was going to turn into two goblins, and that each of those would divide as well, until there were dozens of them who would all come at me, in a cloud. I was so frightened that I couldn't see straight or think straight, which was why it took me several seconds to understand what it was that Henry and I were watching.

What it was, was the new little black cat from the doctors' house, struggling with a young jay, which was so terrified that it had only just got itself together enough to give a recognisable scream.

Without thinking, I ran over and picked up the jay, just as the cat was about to get to grips with it again. It was quite a big bird, but my hands went around it, and I'd got it from behind, so I was holding it the right way up, with its wings in place at its sides. It froze in my hands, and the little cat, with an expression as nasty as any goblin, began to leap up at me to get at it.

I ran the few steps to the back door, and as I got there the light went on in the kitchen, and I yelled, "Let me in," and Mum opened the door, looking startled.

The cat and the jay and I all fell over the doorstep together, leaving Henry shocked on the fence, and I yelled at Mum, "Keep the cat, keep the cat."

Mum was much quicker on the uptake than I'd been. She understood what was happening at once, and didn't ask questions. While I stared at what I could see of the jay in my hands, and noted that it seemed to be complete and that there wasn't any blood, she managed to get me out of the door again, keeping the little black cat inside, which wasn't easy because it was quite manic by then, determined not to let me steal its prey. Mum had to throw the kitchen towel over it as it leapt up at me, and then grab hold of the whole bundle.

The jay was rigid and silent in my hands, and I might have thought it was dead of fright except that it had somehow got its feet clasped over the middle finger of my left hand, and was gripping hard.

As I backed out of the door I just caught a glimpse of a bundle of blue and white towel, spitting and heaving on the floor, with Mum bending over it, and then I took the jay quickly to the end fence.

Henry watched from his distance as I tried to stand the bird on the fence. It wouldn't let go of my finger, though. I think it was in shock. So I took it through the fence and crouched under the nearest apple tree and put it on the ground, with my hands still around it. Then I managed to prise its claws free and get my hands away. It looked undamaged to me, but it was as still as a carving.

I backed slowly away and out through the fence gap and watched it from our side. The big house was quiet and empty again, the Developer had gone, and I knew Henry would be no bother. He only ever chases birds that are quite obviously going to get away.

At first I thought it was going to sit there, frozen, all night, and then die of fright, but after what seemed like hours, and Mum told me later was twenty minutes, it began to stretch its wings a bit, testing them. Then it hopped a few paces. Then it bent its knees and flung itself into the air and flapped up into the lowest boughs of the apple tree. It perched there for a few moments and then it raised its crest and opened its beak and gave a great shriek of rage. Finally, it flew off towards the chestnut tree and vanished, to some safe sleeping place inside, I suppose.

We kept the little black cat for half an hour more. Mum and I discussed the foolishness of young jays who stay out late, and explained to Sam and Dad what all the shouting and slamming of doors had been about. My lip got sympathy and a pill, and the cat scratches on my legs and arms got Savlon. By then, although the cat was still keen to get out of our place, it didn't have murder written all over it any more.

I opened the back door, and it padded off into the night, and when it was well out of the way, Henry came in, his every stripe a frown.

At last I tottered upstairs to confront my homework and it was only, truly, when I got there that I remembered the earlier encounter, the one with the Developer.

Unreal, I thought, it's all unreal. I'll tell them in the morning when I've got it straight in my mind.

I didn't, as it happened. What with homework, and meal times, and Sam being sent back from school with no skin on either of his knees and blood all over his socks, a couple of days went by, and I still hadn't found the right moment.

# CHAPTER ELEVEN

I did not forget the letter from school on purpose. I just forgot it. People do forget things. That's why there's a word for it. But Mum and Dad – both – thought I'd lost it down the bottom of my briefcase because I was worried about giving it to them, and they were both nice about it, and they both said things like, "It doesn't matter, you've given it to us now," and it is completely impossible to argue with people who are determined to forgive you for something you haven't done.

"Look, I've been busy," I said, "I've been delivering leaflets, I've been on bat watch, I've had things on my mind."

In fact that was the wrong thing to say because it turned out the letter was from my class teacher, rabbiting on about me being 'inattentive and lethargic' and wondering if I had any problems, at school or at home, that she ought to know about.

It was the morning Mum doesn't go into the shop, so she had plenty of time to talk about it, and so I suppose had Dad, but luckily I was able to keep saying, "I have to leave in fifteen (ten, five, two) minutes," which cut it short.

"I'm all for you being concerned about what's happening around you," said Mum, "but I'd rather school didn't suffer, that's all."

"OK," I said.

"Are you fretting about the urticaria?" said Dad.

"No more than usual," I said.

"Is there anything else bothering you?" said Mum.

"Just the Developer," I said. "Just him, he's enough," and that's when I told them about meeting him in the garden, and what he'd said about me being selfish.

"I'm sorry to have to say this, Jo," said Mum, "but I'm afraid I agree with him. I quite see that the garden's pretty, and I know you've got a lot of pleasure out of it, but you can't expect to keep it, it isn't yours. You know I don't believe in labelling people – but that man is trying to build houses for other people to live in, while you are trying to stop him so you can go on trespassing and bird watching. Which sounds to you like the Good Guy?"

"Sam has the last word on the Developer," said Dad. "All property is theft."

"Then we're thieves ourselves," said Mum crossly, "we're buying this house, aren't we?"

Sam didn't say anything – he'd already left for school.

"I have to go," I said. By then I really *did* have to.

"We'll talk about it tonight," said Mum, "but just think about this – there's a woman who comes into the shop regularly – very nice – quite elderly – she's always talking about her daughter and son-in-law who can't find a place to buy near her. Think of them – that should help to make it real for you. Think of that young couple wanting a home of their own, and think that perhaps they might buy one of the houses out at the back when it's built, and think how lovely it would be for that woman to have them living nearby, especially as she gets older."

"Not a dry eye in the house," said Dad quietly.

"But," said Mum to me, ignoring him, "I want us to be fair about this, so we're both going to go down to the Town Hall this morning, and by the time you get back from school we'll have seen the plans ourselves, and we can all discuss this properly, knowing what we're talking about. All right?"

"All right," I said.

"First I've heard of it," said Dad.

"It's the first time I've thought of it," said Mum.

"I'm off now," said I.

"And another thing," said Mum, "we're going to start keeping a diary, noting down everything you eat and exactly when the urticaria comes up, and then we'll see if we can work out some kind of diet that cuts it out altogether. It must be more than just chocolate that does it."

"Bye," I said, and I left at a good speed, more or less jogging. Then at the corner I slowed down to my normal walk. 'She' could hardly complain if I was a few minutes late today, considering it was 'her' letter that had caused it. Then I remembered I should have given them the letter as soon as I got in from school yesterday. We should have done our talking about it last night. If 'she' thought I'd held it back till today 'she', too, would decide I was worried about it. I began to jog again.

It's no good thinking about where you're going if you're running late. You just keep remembering how many stretches of the route there are still to do, and then you get seriously depressed. It's better to think of something else.

I tried thinking how selfish I was, not wanting people to have homes to live in. But that wasn't a good thought to jog to.

Then I tried thinking that it truly wasn't only me I cared about, it was also the crows and the squirrels and the trees and – all right, Developer, – the slugs and the spiders and the stinging nettles, too. But that wasn't a new enough idea to carry me down many streets.

I got to the big junction and stopped thinking while I attended to crossing the road. Usually I'm able to do two things at once, but not when one of them might kill me.

When I was on the other side, I had a go at picturing the future.

The house was gone and there was a five-storey block of flats in its place. It looked grim, but then I decorated it with window boxes, full of lobelias and petunias, and it looked a lot better. I hoped the petunias would live a bit longer than our geraniums.

Then I conjured up the little houses. That was hard – it meant I had to flatten the garden first, and I hated doing that so much that I let out a little grunt, and a woman who was hurrying past me jumped slightly and gave me an odd look.

I decided that if the builders were very careful they would be able to put the houses on the lawn and divide up the flower beds and trees into little separate gardens, one each. All right, so I knew there wasn't enough lawn for all the houses, but I wanted to get used to reality gradually.

So next I thought they might build one of the houses between the pergola steps and the orchard, down at our end. (I had to adapt my memory of the garden a bit to make room even for a Wendy house in such a tiny space, but never mind.) That might be the house the young couple would buy, the ones with the old mother who went to Mum's shop, and that way they would get a little garden with an apple tree and a damson tree in it. They could grow honey-suckle and clematis all over their little house, so it would blend in nicely with its surroundings.

I switched off the image while I crossed the last big road before school, and when I switched it on again the little house – which seemed to be the only one that had been built – was looking as pretty as anything. It was late afternoon on a summer day and the old mother was sitting in a garden chair, beside a tiny table, under the apple tree, enjoying the sun and waiting for her daughter to bring out a tray of afternoon tea.

Then I remembered that the sun goes down more or less behind the conservatory of the big house, and that when the massive great block of flats was smashed down on top of it, it would cast a great shadow from quite early in the afternoon.

In my imagination, the sun vanished suddenly and the old woman frowned, shivered, and went indoors for a cardigan.

I'd reached the school gates. I wouldn't let myself look at my watch, but the playground was empty, and anyway you can tell when you're late. It's in the air. I suppose I'd been walking more and more slowly. It takes time to grow honeysuckle all up a new house and to choose the right kind of garden furniture.

While I hung up my coat, I ran the fantasy-time back to twelve noon and I forced the old woman out again onto her little chair, and I brought the sun back, shining down from overhead, well clear of the block. I created her daughter, coming out of the little house carrying a tray of sandwiches, and her son-in-law following with a jug of fruit squash with ice clinking in it and slices of orange and lemon bobbing about.

But just as they approached the table to put the things down on it, all the other small houses suddenly fell out of the sky and crashed down into place all around them, and one hit the end fence of their garden, and knocked over the apple tree, and the tree fell across the little table, and the old woman fell off her chair, and the glass jug shattered ...

And I went into class for a bit of peace and quiet. Not that I found much. I had to listen to a lot of stuff about bad time-keeping, which was very unsettling.

I gloomed my way home after school and went straight up to my room to glare at my homework. I didn't look in on Dad because I didn't feel like chatting, so it wasn't until Mum came back and we all wandered into the kitchen that I found out that everything had changed since the morning.

I don't know what Mum can have been like in the shop in the afternoon because she was still, by six o'clock, in a high old rage about her visit to the Town Hall, and Dad was agreeing with her, though he wasn't quite so wound up as she was. Even Sam was aware something was in the air, and just stood and gaped.

"It's a LUXURY development," said Mum, leaning with her back against the sink and her arms folded. "All that stuff about 'people need houses to live in' – what he means is RICH people need houses to live in' – what he means is he needs to sell houses to rich people so HE can make a good living. I think it's disgusting!"

"Shall I have a go at the potatoes?" said Dad, fussing about beside her with the peeler in one hand, but Mum didn't shift from the sink, I don't think she even heard him.

"That block of flats," she said, "is going to stick out as far as the ornamental conifers – everything in the garden, up to and including them, is going to be wiped out, and it's FIVE STOREYS HIGH."

"I know," I said, and I sat down at the kitchen table.

"It's going to loom over us out at the back there like – like – like . . ."

"Like a block of flats," said Dad. He'd given up thinking about food and he sat at the table, too, and so did Sam. We were like a class of three, listening to teacher.

"They're going to be able to see into all our gardens and into our top windows," said Mum, "and the houses nearest them, up the two side rows, are going to be completely overshadowed. I shouldn't think Sarah or any of them up that end are ever going to see sunlight in their gardens again."

"It will change things," said Dad.

"And the *houses*!" said Mum. "They'll be worse because they're nearer, and they're three-storey, as high as we are, and now I come to think of it I don't suppose any of the rest of us'll ever get sun in our gardens again, either. And we're not old enough to claim Ancient Lights, I checked."

"What does that mean?" I said, as she paused to cough. At first I wondered if Mrs Potts was old enough to claim them, and then I tried to guess what they were. They sounded like something you might find inside a dinosaur.

"It's a legal term," said Dad. "If a house has stood for long enough, then you can't come along and build something that cuts off its light."

"Not unless you're replacing a building that always *used* to cut off its light," said Mum in a calmer voice.

"Anyway," said Dad, "we can't claim it, so they can block off whatever they want to, more or less."

I patted the table top with the palms of my hands, to get their attention. "People need houses to live in!" I said. "That old woman who comes to you for her aspirins, her daughter and son-in-law need a home."

Mum's rage rose again, and she pushed herself off from the sink and then thumped herself back against it again, so that the dishes in the drainer rattled and the washing up liquid fainted against the window.

"They could never afford one of those houses," she said. "I told you, they're for the rich, the Council told us the planned price range. They're not even very big, but they're in London, that's what counts apparently, and they're going to have garages and picture windows, and they all face inwards, with their picture windows looking onto their own courtyard, and mean little windows on the outsides so they don't have to see our scruffy houses and gardens. You should just *see* the plans!"

"I *have*," I said, and I knew it would come out as a wail, in fact I meant it to, but even I was surprised when it came out as a scream.

Mum flopped down at the table with the rest of us and grabbed my nearest hand. "Of course you have, Jo," she said. "I'm sorry. I just had no idea. I still believe what I said before, but it certainly doesn't apply to this development."

It might have been me who forgot about the letter from school last night – tonight it was Mum and Dad who forgot. Never mind discussing diet sheets, never mind about shoving me off to do my homework and talking about sensible bedtimes – we cooked fast, ate fast, burped fast, and then we got down to things. It was great.

Marion Bartlett had got into Mum all right. I hoped Kathleen, wherever she was, didn't feel too lost without her.

"We have to be careful here," said Mum, "we can't expect to stop them developing, not now they've bought it, but we can try and make them do it carefully."

So we wrote a steaming letter to the Council, which Mum and Dad both signed, saying we thought the house should be saved and turned into flats, with guaranteed bat accommodation in the rafters; we thought the new houses should be lower, two-storey instead of three, and also we thought there should be fewer of them so that the nice features of the garden – especially the big trees and the orchard – could be saved. We even pointed out that this would make things a whole lot nicer for the newcomers when they moved in.

Then we looked at my spare copy of the leaflet I'd delivered, begging everyone to write, and sort of telling them what they might like to say, and we did a PS leaflet which told them, in case they hadn't seen the plans, that this was to be luxury accommodation for the rich – and that people who had enough money to buy houses at that price could perfectly well go and live somewhere else.

Next I rang the bat-man and convinced him of what I'd seen, and he said he'd come over in the next couple of days, or nights rather, and report his findings to the Council.

Finally, we set off around the block, Mum and Sam going in one direction and Dad and me in the other, and bunged our PS leaflets through all the doors. (Mum got Mrs Potts's street, and Sam managed to get both watches right for her – her own and the quartz one – for the time being, anyway. She let him set them for her. She said she didn't mind him doing it because 'boys know about these things', which pleased Sam and made Mum and me a bit shirty.)

Then we collapsed back home. Mr Penn had told Mum

and Dad that the Planning Application would come up in front of the Council in three weeks' time, so Mum said we could relax now, and I could concentrate on school. Dad said that being a caring member of the community was very tiring and time consuming and did we all realise it was nearly eleven o'clock. Sam just yawned. Poor old Sam, I don't think he really grasped, at that point, what we were all on about, but he joined in without complaining.

I looked forward to telling Kathleen that I had, after all, mobilised a private army, and that everything was going to be all right now. Funny how I kept thinking everything was going to be all right.

# CHAPTER TWELVE

The young crows still lived in the garden, though they were as big as their parents. But big as they were, they vanished completely on what had once been the lawn but was now a kind of meadow. If anything walked across it all I could see were waving grasses – is it a bird? Is it a breeze? No it's super-squirrel!

The golden rod had gone totally wild, spreading all over its own bed and carrying right on out amongst the grass. The fat pink roses had opened on the old pergola bush. The honeysuckle and creeper were thick and leafy, all over the back of the house, and were beginning to grow across the windows. They must have had to cut them back every year, I hadn't realised.

Dad came back from his round-the-block jogging sessions with reports on the front of the house which he said was vanishing behind the wisteria and creeper. He said it looked like Sleeping Beauty's castle. In fact the whole house and garden now looked completely demented, though in a nice, friendly kind of way.

The spindly troughs and the tubs on the patio stayed empty and there was nothing at all in the greenhouse to fill them up with. I suppose Mr and Mrs Owner had taken all the moveable plants with them wherever they'd gone – or perhaps they were, even now, flowering on the Developer's own patio. I could bet he had a big garden.

In our little garden the hydrangea was shoving out some quite nice flowers – rather a washy pink colour, but good and fat, while the geraniums up the side alley were practising to be compost, and getting quite good at it.

The bat-man had called us to say there was definitely a bat roost in the attic of the house, and that he'd made the necessary reports. A family of hedgehogs had begun to trundle around like tanks at the bottom of the garden, making so much noise we could hear them from our side, grumbling and sniffing. It must be awful to have all those fleas and all those prickles and no way you can use the one to scratch the other.

Then a man carrying a large cardboard box with air holes punched in it had climbed over Mr Dahlia's fence and called and made clicking noises for a while, and at last the pretty brown pigeon had flown down to him. He'd packed it carefully in the box and taken it away. I saw him shaking hands with Mr Dahlia, after he'd climbed back over his fence. Dad said it must have been a ringed racing pigeon on an unscheduled holiday.

Apart from that, there was no real excitement out the back.

My diet-urticaria diary was turning out to be quite useful. Cheese had to be avoided, we'd found, and so had nuts. Mum had always been suspicious of tomatoes (which Sam said you could tell were poisonous just by looking at them) so she'd withheld them for a time, and then she'd given me a lot of home-made tomato soup followed by egg and tomato salad for supper.

Next morning Dad said I looked like a boxer who hadn't quite got the hang of self-defence. My eyes were so swollen, above and below, that I had to point the mean little slits directly at whatever I wanted to look at. My bulging lips stuck out so far I could actually see them without using a mirror, even with my limitations, and the pattern of blobs on my back and shoulders had joined up till I was one big blob.

Mum was highly delighted. "*Now* we're getting somewhere," she said.

"Oh good," I said, and began to cry.

Mum was severe at first, said I shouldn't make a fuss about something that wasn't life-threatening.

I said it was life-threatening, because if I had to go to school looking like that, I'd throw myself under a bus on the way.

Mum got a bit nicer and said she didn't expect me to go anywhere until it had gone down – in fact she would ring the school and say I wouldn't be in till tomorrow.

So that's why I was there that afternoon, lying on my bunk squinting puffily at a book, listening to Kathleen's typewriter above me and Dad's occasional telephone calls down below. Henry lay beside me, but not on me. He's a good sick visitor, knows how to be companionable without getting itchily close.

Dad had completely stopped twitching about having Kathleen in the house. She had never, ever, gone into his office, and she had, he told us, twice answered the front door, once to a Jehovah's Witness and once to someone wanting jumble, and had got rid of them without letting on he was at home. She had even earned his highest praise of all – "She's the kind of person," he'd said, "you can meet in the kitchen when you're both making coffee, and not have to start a conversation with." Also, she was away a lot.

Everything was peaceful except for the sound of an electric lawn mower. I hadn't heard one of those since the big house became empty, and I wondered vaguely whose it was. Even the two houses each side of the big house only had small bits of grass, and people seemed to push old fashioned mowers around on those. I decided the doctors were the most likely ones to have splashed out on a powered one, and I got up to look.

## Chapter Twelve

The first thing I noticed was that the pine tree – which had always stood further into the garden than the other big trees – seemed to have moved a little further forward still, which was strange. Then, as I looked at it, it swayed to and fro and then sank sideways, very slowly, across the garden, and as it sank one of its branches caught hold of the pergola, and they fell down together, and bounced slightly, and lay still, with the fat pink roses tumbling all over them - almost like a wreath.

In the gap where the pine tree had stood I could see two men, one of them holding an electric saw on a long lead. They clambered over the body of the tree and began to walk down the garden towards the little orchard.

Perhaps I could have moved faster, but I didn't really believe what was happening.

The crows took to the air, and for once their angry harsh voices sounded right. A magpie flew from nowhere and landed on our fence and stood with its back to me, shrieking and swearing at the two men who were walking through the garden, one of them trailing the saw behind him like a toy. I don't think the men even knew the bird was there.

Shouting did seem the only answer.

As I reached the landing outside my bedroom, Kathleen came stumbling down the stairs from her attic, quite white-faced, and Dad came out of his office and started to run up the stairs. I think they both thought I was being attacked, and it was a few minutes before I could make them understand – which in the end I did by running to my window and pointing, as if I was a dog or something. By that time the saw was buzzing again, and a damson fell in seconds, snapped off just above the roots as if it was nothing bigger than a foxglove.

"Can they *do* that?" said Kathleen.

"Apparently," said Dad, as the men stepped over the damson and stood by the apple tree next to it, one of them using the saw, the other leaning on the little tree above

135

saw-height to push it in the direction they wanted it to fall.

"All right," said Kathleen – "quickly – one of us goes and rings the Council and the other two go and talk to the men."

"You ring the Council," said Dad wearily, "take Joanna to the phone, she'll get you the number."

I didn't feel offended that I wasn't expected to ring – I couldn't even speak properly to them, no one would have been able to understand me over the telephone.

Kathleen and I ran to the office. It was the first time she'd been in it, but she didn't look around, just took the telephone receiver from me when I'd got Mr Penn on the line, and told him, shortly and sharply, what was happening and where.

Dad had gone out of back door, but the awful, evil, mowing noises of the saw went on and on and on.

"Well, you'll have to be quick," said Kathleen, down the line, "there are trees going now, while I'm telling you, electric saws work fast."

When she hung up, she nodded to me. "They're coming down," she said. "Someone's going to ring the Developer's office, and someone's coming along here. How far is the Town Hall?"

"Far enough," I said. "They can kill a tree while he finds his car keys, kill a tree while he runs to the car park, kill a tree while he starts up ..."

"Come on," said Kathleen briskly. "Let's go out back and talk to them."

I didn't want to, I can't explain how much I didn't want to. I didn't want to see what was out there any more than I'd have wanted to see a road accident, but I had to follow her.

As we got outside the buzzing stopped at last and I could see Dad in the garden, talking to the saw-man and the other. Kathleen and I slid through the fence-gap to join him, and the four of them had a long meaningless conversation, that I couldn't concentrate on. The two men with the saw were saying that they were only doing their job, they were just obeying orders, all that sort of stuff. Dad and Kathleen were talking about the Council, and Planning Permission, and various Laws of the Land which I think they were making up as they went along. I knew they were just playing for time, hoping to keep the talking going until help arrived. Everyone else seemed to be at work or school. The only other neighbour to come out was Mr Dahlias but he just stood at his fence and stared. The Fusspots' curtains twitched a bit, but that was all. I expect the bird lady was under her duvet with her fingers in her ears – where I'd like to have been.

You wouldn't believe what they'd done in those minutes while Kathleen and I had telephoned and Dad had shouted to make himself heard above the row. Those little old orchard trees had quite thin stems and ten of them – ten – lay on the ground, at all angles, in a scattering of dropped half-grown apples and the tiny beginnings of plums. There were only three left standing, including the one where I'd left the rescued jay, and the man with the saw was leaning on that one.

The pine looked tragic, all mixed up with the rose like it was. I knew it was silly of me, but I kept thinking it had grabbed at the rose-pergola as it fell, to try to save itself, and that it was sorry it had pulled the pergola down with it when it went.

I worked my way over towards it, and I could see the crows' nest – a tatty old mass of twigs that they'd renovated year after year – still in the top branches. I could hear a crow voice. I looked up and Father Crow was on the roof of the house, making a terrible row. I couldn't see any of the others.

The old rose still had its roots in the earth, and though it had fallen down completely it didn't seem to be very damaged. But the tree was lost. To walk to the top of it I had to go more than half way across the garden, away from where its roots were, towards Mrs Potts's side. I had to climb a little damson that was lying on its side with two of its branches broken under it. When I got to the pine I touched it and told it I was sorry. I told it I felt I should have been able to save it, but that I didn't know how. Perhaps if I'd seen them coming I could have gone out and stood in front of it, but I'm not sure if I'd have had the courage. All I could do now was stand there uselessly, all puffy and revolting as I was, and sympathise with it.

They don't die at once, when they're cut down – it was still alive – it takes a while before the branches understand that the trunk is cut off from the roots. It looked so surprised. Shocked, really.

Then I went round the apples and the damsons. I had to say some sort of goodbye, I thought. I didn't look at any of the trees that were still standing – in a situation like that you'd want to reassure a standing tree, but I didn't know if I reasonably could.

At last Mr Penn turned up, with two other men, both carrying clipboards, and they all came into the garden through the house. As he came onto the terrace, Mr Penn stopped still for a moment, and then he carried on walking towards the fallen trees. Just as I was wondering how he and the others had got in, and thinking that perhaps the saw-men had left the door open, the Developer himself appeared in the french windows and came marching down the garden behind them. As soon as he saw us, of course, he started going on about trespassers, and then he began to shout at Mr Penn – who looked awfully young at that moment, even to me – telling him that he was supposed to be impartial and here he was, obviously in collusion with the neighbours.

"Not at all," said Kathleen loudly, "we just came through to check if these trees were really supposed to be felled. I can assure you that I've never seen any of these people" – and she waved at Mr Penn and the others – "before this moment." Then she turned away and said to Dad and me,

"Let's get inside. We're going to make things tough all round if we stay out here and try to join in."

Dad, who I don't think had ever confronted anyone before in all his life, was glad to go in. So was I. I'd seen enough of dying bodies to last me forever.

We watched from my bedroom, Kathleen and I, and there was a lot of shouting and pointing and measuring and note-taking. Then the saw-men left, and Mr Penn and the others talked on for ages. During all this, Sam got home and came into my room to see what was going on. I wasn't pleased to see him at first – I thought he'd find it all very exciting, and I didn't think I could stand that – but dear old Sam, he didn't, he went a sort of greenish colour and just stared. Then he asked where Henry was.

"He's OK, he's in the kitchen," I said.

When they'd all left the garden, which looked as though a small tornado had gone through it, we allowed Mr Penn thirty minutes to get back to his desk and then Kathleen rang him and Dad and Sam and I all sat around in the study listening. Kathleen repeated everything Mr Penn said, the way they do in plays sometimes, if they want the audience to know what's happening on the other end of the line.

She said things like, "You say you've put Preservation Orders on the rest of the trees?" and, "you say you'll prosecute, but you don't know that that'll achieve much."

From what she said over the phone like that, and from what she explained after she'd hung up, it seemed that the Council had turned down the Developer's original Planning Application, and had asked him to submit a revised one that would save the larger trees and also the house – on account of the bats. They had not, said Mr Penn, seen any way of saving the orchard, which was in any case quite old, but they were amazed, even so, that the Developer should have gone ahead and cut stuff down until he had got a 'planning brief' approved. The pine should not have been felled, and they would prosecute him for taking it down, which would mean he would be fined. But Developers expect that, said Mr Penn, and when they work out their costings they often allow for paying fines on a few good trees that are in their way.

When the new application was submitted, we'd be informed, as before, and we could go and see what we thought of it.

"And if you don't like it," Mr Penn had said, "you'll have to start the protests all over again from scratch, you can't carry them over to a new application."

He also said that now they'd done the cutting they would be allowed to clear the site – which would probably mean chopping wood and lighting a bonfire or two.

We drifted off to the middle room afterwards, all feeling a bit vacant and shaky and unsure what to do next.

"Cheer up," said Kathleen after a bit, "you've made a mark already. You've saved the house."

I said, "I don't care about the house. It's the garden I love, what's left of it."

Then I felt mean, because the house is a nice old thing, and has bats, and also Kathleen said, "If they're keeping the house, they'll have to keep the bit of garden nearest to it, they can't build right up to its windows. And maybe all this has given the Developer a shock – maybe he now realises he can't do just what he likes – maybe his new plans will be for something you're happy with."

"Maybe," I said.

The front door opened and in came Mum. "It's been a grisly day," she said. "Wall-to-wall hypochondriacs. Oh good, Jo, your swellings have gone down. That's nice, I could do with some good news."

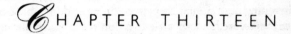

# CHAPTER THIRTEEN

When I look back, it seems to me that it was the pine tree being cut down that began the change, but it wasn't really. It must really have all begun with a conversation between Mr and Mrs Owner, months ago, while the rest of us were thinking about other things, with no idea that they were discussing the house and garden and how much they'd make if they sold them. I don't suppose many things really do happen suddenly, even if they seem to. I expect most things creep up on you from months and months away – it's just that you don't see them coming.

Once the change began, though, it didn't stop. Everything, at that time, seemed to be about disappointment and destruction.

The electric saws went on all day, for days on end. It took much longer to cut up the trees than it had taken to cut them down. Even though they were dead, I hated to see them being butchered, and I didn't look out much, but Sam – who did – said they took away the big logs. The rest they piled up for a bonfire.

They built the bonfire on the stone steps between what had been the orchard and what had been the lawns. It gave them a firm dry place to start off on, which they needed because the wood was green and full of sap and hard to burn. The rock plants which were nearest to the fire went brown and shrivelled, and even the ones further away withered in the heat and smoke. If the Council couldn't see a way of saving the orchard, it obviously wouldn't be able to save the saxifrage and aubretia, so there wasn't any point complaining about what they were doing. I don't think they knew they were being heartless. I think they only saw what they were doing – clearing up. I don't think they were aware of the plants at all.

The green burning wood made angry snapping, cracking noises and gave off explosions of red sparks which glittered like fierce red eyes against the thick column of grey smoke. They weren't supposed to light the fire if the wind would blow the smoke over any of our houses, but they did. I don't think they were aware of us, either. We were allowed to complain about the smoke, but by the time we'd rung the Council, and by the time the Council had sent someone down to see about it, we were already kippered, and the men were letting the fire die out for the evening anyway. Perhaps they were told not to do it again, but if they were they forgot what they'd been told by next day.

All we could do, Sam and I, was go through the fence each morning, very early, before the men arrived, and kick and shout around the pile of branches they'd stacked on the steps, to try and frighten away any hedgehogs or mice who might be sleeping in there, and who might not manage to get out in time when the flames started. Sam was always very quiet when we first went in, not like himself at all, but the shouting and kicking cheered him up. I don't know if anyone from any of the other houses saw us, and if they did I don't know if they thought we were mad, or vandals, or if they guessed what we were doing.

The squirrels stayed around, and I still saw the bats in the evenings. I suppose they were another reason for building the fire down on the steps, away from the house, because the men had understood that they mustn't frighten the bats away.

# Chapter Thirteen

The odd thing was the birds. All the smaller ones became nervous and cautious, so that I hardly saw them at all, while the big brave ones – the jays and magpies and crows – weren't too much affected. Looking out in the early evening, when the smoke was dying down and the men were gone, it seemed that only the carrion birds were still around. I was glad the crow family had stayed on, and I hoped the parent birds would build a new nest in another tree next spring, but they looked so horribly suitable in the damaged garden that I had to be careful not to let myself go off them.

One day, when the men had sawn and burnt their way through most of the fallen trees, and had broken up the rotting shed beside my stump and cheered up the bonfire by throwing that on, too, Sam and I happened to look out of my window. We watched as they set off towards the rose, which had been flowering away quite happily on the ground ever since it had fallen off the broken pergola.

We should have run out and stopped them, but they were so quick, and we couldn't have known what they were going to do, it isn't the sort of thing you'd think of in the normal way. What they did was they cut through the old, old stem in about three seconds, and then between them they picked up the whole bush and carried it, with its stem and branches trailing and waving all around them, and threw the whole thing on the fire, just like that, flowers and buds and all, and the fire was burning quite strongly when they did it, and even from where we were we could see that all the roses shrivelled in two seconds, and the bush kind of sank down comfortably into the flames, and within about thirty more seconds you wouldn't have known it had ever been a rose bush, you'd have thought it was just a bit of garden rubbish. Well – it was just a bit of garden rubbish by the time they'd done with it.

"They could have picked the flowers," said Sam. "Why didn't they pick the flowers?"

It wasn't that Sam had changed completely, he still spent

most of his time upside down or on the move, but he did look at things more carefully now, I noticed, and he seemed to have a much better idea of what was going on than before. It was just a shame that what was going on was so grim.

We couldn't forgive them for the rose. We'd kept thinking the trees weren't their fault, they were just doing what the Developer said they had to, but they could have taken the rose home, or given it to one of the other gardens, or at least – as Sam said – picked the flowers first.

"I expect they've got thorns in their fingers," said Sam, "they must have, and they won't have bothered to get them out, and the thorns will have worked their way in, right up their arms and into their lungs and hearts and stuff, and they'll go septic, and it'll hurt, and then they'll die. Don't you think, Jo?"

"No, I don't" I said. "But it's a great idea."

In the end that wasn't the worst thing they did, but I suppose the other really wasn't their fault.

While all this was going on, Kathleen took a trip to the Midlands cousins and came back with Marion Bartlett's 'effects' as she called them. She had been so keen to get hold of the things, so afraid that the cousins wouldn't get around to looking them out, that I expected her to come back all excited, like she had when she'd discovered the extra relatives' name on the Scottish gravestone, but she wasn't like that, in fact she didn't seem particularly happy at all.

I didn't guess the reason at first. Partly I was too busy being good about not demanding to see the stuff at once. Marion Bartlett was Kathleen's before she was mine, and I thought she might like to gloat over the letters, or whatever she'd been given, for a while before she had to share them. Also, we were all depressed, so it didn't seem surprising that Kathleen was the same.

On her second evening back, she invited me up to her attic to see the special package. I could understand why she

## Chapter Thirteen

wouldn't want to show it off in front of Mum and Dad. You didn't need to be especially perceptive to see that they weren't interested. Also, they had decided to be a bit peeved that the distant Midlands cousins hadn't sent down any kind of message or greeting.

I said, "I expect it runs in the family, I expect they don't want to get involved with us, either," but Mum just said, "That's not the point." When she gets political like that it's best not to argue.

It was a very little package indeed that Kathleen put down on her duvet between us. "It's just a few letters," she said, "that's all. No photos. And the writing's very pretty, but it's also very hard to read. I'll type them out over the next few days to make it easier. Also," she made a face, "I'm afraid they're a bit damaged. They were found in Marion's daughter's cottage in the country and mice had been using them to nest in. Co-existing with wildlife isn't always ideal, it seems."

I slid the letters, what was left of them, out of their package, very carefully. She had had nice writing, Marion, strong like I'd have expected, but Kathleen was right, it wasn't easy to read, and I felt very discouraged when I saw that most of the pages had chunks chomped out of them, so that even if you could read the words, you wouldn't often be able to finish a whole sentence.

"Have you read them?" I said, because although I really was very excited to think I was holding letters that Marion Bartlett herself had actually written, I admit I felt a bit lazy about ploughing through them.

"Bits of them," said Kathleen. "Well, most of them, really, but it'll be easier after I've typed them. At the moment I find that by the time I've deciphered the end of a sentence, I've forgotten how it started."

"Do they tell us anything more?" I said.

"Yes," said Kathleen, just like that, and I suppose that's when I began to guess.

'What, then?" I said.

"It didn't all happen quite as we thought," said Kathleen cautiously. She looked terribly worried. She seemed to feel very guilty about whatever it was she had to tell me. I tried to help her out.

"OK, so start at the beginning," I said. "Did she run away to Canada with the missionaries?"

"She went to Canada," said Kathleen, "at about the time we thought – but she didn't actually run away. She met Fred Bartlett when he was over here on a visit and they married in this country and then she went back to Canada with him."

"That doesn't sound too intrepid," I said.

"It *was* a whirlwind romance," said Kathleen hastily. "I don't know where the missionaries came in, if they did at all. I haven't found anything yet – but she and Fred *were* very religious and probably quite evangelical in their way."

"So she didn't go to the North West Territories on her own," I said, "she went with Fred. Is that what you're trying to tell me?"

"Yes," said Kathleen doubtfully.

"You mean she didn't go to the North West Territories at all?" I said. I knew I was beginning to sound a bit shirty. I wanted to be easy-going about all this for Kathleen's sake, but there are limits.

"Well, first of all," said Kathleen, "it seems they went to Toronto and set up home there. But in one of these letters to her sister, Marion does refer back to a trip she and Fred took up in that direction. She doesn't seem to have experienced the winter – or the thaw and the floods – though she does mention the Indians briefly," she stopped sounding wistful and put on a more positive voice, "but then most of her letters are lost," she said, "and we can't expect to find mention of every single thing she did in these few bits of mouse-bedding that survive."

"And that's all?" I said.

"I'm afraid so," said Kathleen. "All the other bits of

information are rather domestic. Fred *was* killed in a railway accident, and she did bring her daughters back over here afterwards. Of course there are other places I can look for more details. Something may turn up in Fred's effects, if we ever track those down."

I put the letters back in their envelope. They hardly seemed worth saving, to me, but they were Kathleen's, not mine. "That's how things are at the moment," I said. "Everything's going wrong and collapsing and being spoilt. I should have guessed Marion Bartlett would turn out to be a fake."

"Oh no!" said Kathleen, taking the letters. "Oh no, no! Poor Marion, you mustn't think that. She wasn't any sort of fake – *she* never said she did any of these things. She just lived her life, and then people began to attach stories to her, and the stories grew. None of it was her doing – and after all, some of the stories may turn out to be true, we don't know yet."

"*I* know," I said. "She was just ordinary."

"I feel so guilty," said Kathleen unhappily. "I passed the stories on to you without checking them first. That was very wrong of me. I just thought they might help."

"It's OK," I said. "It doesn't matter."

I couldn't think of anything else to say, and I didn't know how to change the subject, so I went out of the room. I went quite slowly, so Kathleen wouldn't think I was storming off in a temper or anything, and I went to my room and looked out of the window. Above me, I could hear Kathleen beginning to type. I thought it was no wonder I hadn't saved the garden, me with ordinary old Marion Bartlett's blood in me.

Henry was crouching on our fence, half behind the hydrangea, watching the bonfire. I wondered what he thought about it all.

One of the men picked up a long bendy bit of pine tree and threw it at the fire from the far side. It kind of skimmed the top of it and knocked most of the pile of burning wood down the steps and onto the grass below, and at the same time the flames caught at the green pine and it began to crackle and chatter like a magpie. A stream of orange sparks and black smoke came out of it, straight towards Henry. I don't know if a spark burnt him, or if the smoke got in his eyes, but he turned and sprang off the fence and ran at top speed towards the back door, which must have been open. At that exact moment I heard the front door – Dad said later he'd just been going out to catch the last post – and two seconds after that I heard a horrible mixture of noises – car brakes, tyres skidding, a car horn blasting twice.

By the time I got to the front door there was a woman half falling through our gate towards Dad. She seemed to be crying, and she was saying, "I'm sorry, it just ran out, I'm sorry, it ran right in front of me, it was so quick, I am so sorry . . ."

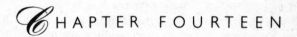

# CHAPTER FOURTEEN

At first I was quite sure Henry was dead, and I think I probably started to cry straightaway, but then I realised that Dad was saying, "Did you see which way?" And the woman was pointing and saying, "It can't have gone far, I hit it such a crack ..."

I was sure she hadn't been able to help what had happened, but I hated her for saying 'it'. She couldn't have known Henry was a 'he', but talking about 'it' seemed horribly final, like talking about 'the body'.

We were all jammed into the hall by then, just like the day Kathleen arrived, and we all rushed out to search in different directions. It was Mum who found him, almost at once, in the narrow front garden of the house right opposite. When she came out from behind the little low front wall, I could see she was carrying him, wrapped in her cardigan.

We gathered round – all except Dad who went straight to the car to start the engine. I think the woman offered her own car as an ambulance, but we shooed her on her way.

Henry looked awful. He looked like a different cat. His fur, the bits of it I could see, was standing on end and all dull, and he'd somehow developed instant dandruff. His eyes didn't seem able to see any of us, he was growling in his throat, and there was blood coming through the cardigan. Dad leaned across the car and opened the passenger door,

Mum got in with Henry, Sam shut the door on them, and they drove off.

I understood that it was vital to get Henry to the vet at once, but it was awful to be left standing there, not knowing how bad he was or if we'd ever see him again.

Kathleen, Sam and I went inside again and shut the door. Sam's teeth were chattering. I felt really sorry for him. I felt sorry for Henry, I felt sorry for myself, I felt sorry for all of us, even for the woman who'd been driving the car.

"Will he be all right?" I said to Kathleen. I don't know why I expected her to know.

"Let's hope so," said Kathleen.

"You don't think the vet'll put him to sleep?" I said, hoping Kathleen would dismiss that idea at once.

But she just said, "The vet will try to save him, they always do. But if he can't be saved then it's best he doesn't suffer for any longer than he has to."

We went into the middle room and put the television on and sat in a row and stared at it. I don't know what we saw. We heard the car pull up outside after about half an hour, and we went to the door again. Mum and Dad were on their own. Mum had the cardigan rolled up in a lump in her hand. I began to feel sick, but then she called out, "So far, so good. Keep your fingers crossed."

It seemed that Henry's back leg was badly broken and the vet was going to operate directly after surgery to see what she could do about it. He'd have to stay in while it healed, and also so that he could be kept under observation in case of internal injuries. But the vet had said she was hopeful. She'd told Mum and Dad he was a strong, healthy cat and she thought he'd come through it.

"He didn't look like Henry," I said, "when you went off with him."

"A lot of that was pain and fear," said Mum. "Shock, really. We just have to hope for the best. Let's assume he's going to be all right unless we're told he's not."

# Chapter Fourteen

I think we had some supper. I don't remember that bit. I just remember waiting until ten o'clock when the vet had said we could ring in to see how the emergency op. had gone.

Mum looked a bit more cheerful when she came back from the phone. Henry was still unconscious from the anaesthetic, she said, but he'd got through the operation very well, good strong heart beat, no signs of giving way yet. The leg had been tidied up and set, and as far as anyone could tell at this stage there was no other damage, but we would just have to wait and see. We could ring again tomorrow – in fact we could ring as often as we liked – but he wouldn't be able to come home for quite a little while. The vet didn't break it to us straightaway that 'quite a little while' meant at least a month.

I had to tap so many things so many times that I began to feel seriously tired, but I didn't mind, I just wanted Henry to be OK and the tapping and the counting was the only thing I could think of to do that might help. I was hardly bothering with fives at all, by then, it was always at least twenty-five – and quite often I had to tap twenty-five times with each foot, each hand and then my tongue – five times twenty-five. The harder it was to do it all without being noticed, the more effective I felt it would be, and each time I got through a session I imagined his broken bones joining together a little bit more surely, his bruises fading a little bit faster.

The vet had said we could visit him if we wanted to, but that in her experience visits unsettled 'hospitalised' animals – they always expected to be taken home at the end of the visit and were disappointed all over again when they were left behind. We thought about it and decided not to go, though Sam had awful misgivings. "He'll think we don't care about him," he kept saying, "he doesn't know we ring up every day."

Henry took our minds off everything else, and when the letter came from the Council to say that new plans had been submitted for the development of the house and garden, none of use took much interest, and we somehow didn't get round to going to the Town Hall to look at them.

A couple of afternoons later, when we'd heard that Henry was 'coming along nicely', and when Sam had just finished explaining his theories about the Channel Tunnel to me, Kathleen came to invite me to her attic. (Sam'd worked out, he said, that if they collected all the earth and rock they dug out of the tunnel, and dumped it in the Channel, it would fill up the Channel, and then they could build a road across and they wouldn't need the Tunnel after all.) We shared the idea with Kathleen, and then she told me she'd finished typing up Marion's letters and there was one she thought I'd like to see.

I'd rather lost interest in old Marion Bartlett, but I climbed the stairs anyway. I don't know what I thought Kathleen might have discovered, but I certainly didn't expect it to be what it was.

I sat on the edge of her bed and she sat at the little desk Dad had lent her from his office, the one he used to use for bills, and she handed me one of the letters, with its fancy writing and its mouse-eaten corner, and then a sheet of white paper with two paragraphs typed on it. "It's part of a letter to her sister," she said.

I read the typed version first and then – to give myself time to think what to say – I read the original, which was quite easy once I knew what it said. What it said was:

"I don't consider myself to be a superstitious woman, yet I do perform certain rituals, of my own devising, in moments of anxiety. I'm sure it's very foolish, but it does make me feel better.

"However, when Fred and I made our little expedition up towards the Mackenzie River I confess that these magical precautions of mine threatened to become more of a problem than the dangers I sought to avert. Certainly the land is barren and challenging, and although the only Indians we encountered were courteous and friendly, and although we travelled in the brief summertime and thus avoided the harsh conditions of winter, and the even more terrifying floods of the great spring thaw, nevertheless we were all the time mindful that we were far from the accustomed safeguards of civilisation. But now I believe that, while a little protective magic may help to strengthen the courage and the will, it is likely that too much may be as poisonous as too strong a dose of an otherwise benign medicine."

As soon as I looked up, and before I had time to say anything, Kathleen said, "You see? She had a similar compulsion to yours. Of course it's not clear if she felt she had to touch things a certain number of times, as you do, but 'magical precautions' obviously run in the family."

You can't give up such a big secret as easily as that, so I started to say something about not knowing what she meant, but Kathleen just went on, "Don't worry, you're very discreet. I doubt if anyone else knows. But you see I had the same thing myself when I was about your age, so I recognised it."

I think I still went on spluttering a bit, but Kathleen just said, "My number was seven," and I heard myself say, "Mine's five, except it often has to be twenty-five to make it stronger."

Kathleen nodded. "My ultimate best was forty-nine," she said, "even worse!"

By then of course there was no point arguing any more, so I just said, "Do you think it works?" It felt really strange, to talk about it just like that.

"I'm sure it doesn't have any effect on the outside world," said Kathleen, "but I think it can make you feel a bit more confident – until it gets out of hand, that is, and then it takes you over and wears you down."

I handed the letter and the copy back to her and she put it carefully in a folder, among the rest.

"How do you stop it getting out of hand?" I said, as

casually as I could.

"You can't," said Kathleen, without hesitating. "It always does. It's like Frankenstein's monster – you invent it, and then it turns out to be too strong for you."

I wondered how she could say such alarming things in such a calm voice. "So what do you do?" I squeaked.

"You have to stop, I'm afraid," said Kathleen. Once it's no longer useful, once it starts to make you feel worse instead of better, you have to ditch it."

The very mention of ditching it seemed to make it stronger than ever. Even though Kathleen knew about it, I still felt I had to hide it from her, and I sort of stared at her in silence, feeling as though my eyes were bulging and my face was turning red as I twitched my toes and fingers and rattled my tongue around my teeth. Kathleen, though, just took all the Marion Bartlett letters and copies out of their folder and began to rearrange them. They were so neat when she began that I was sure it wasn't necessary – I was sure she was doing it so that I would know she wasn't watching me. "The point is," she said, "to stop worrying about it and just let it go. If you grit your teeth and make a resolution never to do it again, you'll find you can't think of anything else. The important thing is that it isn't important, if you see what I mean. It's no big deal. Lots of people do it at some stage in their lives."

"The trouble is," I said, "it's a bad time to stop, right now."

"Of course," said Kathleen. "It always is."

"But it's Henry," I said. "Suppose it does work – suppose I can help him to get better by doing it – then it isn't fair to him to stop, is it?"

Kathleen shuffled the papers, carefully and slowly, putting them out of order, I'm sure, and then back into order again. "Do you really and honestly think the number of times you blink at something can affect the skill of the vet or Henry's own natural healing processes?" she said.

"Not really," I said, "not if you put it like that. But suppose – just suppose – it can?"

"Then keep doing it," said Kathleen. "You're not doing anyone any harm by doing it – keep on with it."

"But it's getting worse already," I said. "What if it goes on getting worse still."

"Oh it will," said Kathleen. "It does, until it stops. But you see the interesting thing is that trying to stop it strengthens it as much as carrying on with it does."

"So how do I ever get out of it?"

"Partly by talking about it," said Kathleen. "The more you try to explain it the sillier it sounds and that weakens its power wonderfully. But mostly by not minding about it. Do it or don't do it, it doesn't matter. It *really* doesn't matter. And things that don't matter don't have power. Do you see?"

She did look at me then. She'd run out of things to do with her papers, I think.

"You see," I said, "I'm worried about Henry."

"Of course you are," said Kathleen. "I'd hope so. Unfortunately, fear and worry strengthen its grip on you, but on the other hand it's natural to be concerned about a sick animal – even one who's getting better every day. If you think it might help Henry, do it. No problem."

"I don't decide to do it," I said. "It isn't as if it's up to me. It tells me what to do."

"Oh I know," said Kathleen. "I remember it well. So – obey or don't. It simply doesn't matter."

"What if people notice?"

"That doesn't matter either."

"They'll think I'm mad."

"No, they'll just think you're a bit twitchy. Unless they recognise what you're up to, in which case they'll understand."

"When did you notice? Today?"

"Oh, on the first evening," said Kathleen. "You were

trying to take an apple after supper, but you had to touch all the others five times before you could. Mind you, I didn't know what the exact number was. Like I said, you're very discreet."

"It's all that Marion Bartlett's fault," I said, suddenly wanting to be angry with someone. "I inherited it from her."

"We might have," said Kathleen. "I know that's what I said. But in fact it's really quite common. Most people have some kind of superstition on the go, whether they admit it or not. But most of them go for the conventional stuff – avoid ladders and the number thirteen – people like us, on the other hand, are more inventive."

I said, "I wonder what Marion did?"

"She doesn't spell it out in any of these letters," said Kathleen. "And *I* wonder what she'd have said if she could have known she'd become a superstition herself. I do feel guilty about that, Joanna. Using her as a talisman and then passing her on to you. I thought you might be able to substitute her for the touching things, you see, but of course a talisman gets just as out of hand as a compulsion, especially when it turns out the poor woman wasn't quite what I thought she was anyway."

"Withhold the taliswoman," I said.

"Indeed!" said Kathleen.

Down in the hall the doorbell rang, long and loudly, and we both jumped.

"People never come at this time," I said, "not at suppertime. Oh – except Sarah when she thought Dad was beating me up." I did hope this visitor didn't have anything to do with me, or Dad would think I was bringing the whole world to his door. I blinked five times, to make it not my fault – (only five, because it wasn't *that* important) – and Kathleen followed me out on to the attic landing to listen over the stairs.

We heard the door open, we heard Dad's voice, we heard

him – after a bit of chat – letting someone in, and then, down in our hall, we heard an unmistakeable voice. He was using his polite, kindly tone, which I'd only encountered once, and Dad and Kathleen not at all, but even so there was no doubt at all who it was. It was the Developer down there, following Dad through in to our middle room; we were being invaded by the enemy.

# CHAPTER FIFTEEN

The Developer sat in Dad's chair in the middle room, so Dad and Mum sat on the sofa, and Sam sat there with them instead of on the floor as usual, and Kathleen ended up on Mum's chair, which left me sitting on the low table on top of the *Radio* and *TV Times*. He'd been in the house two minutes and already he'd managed to muddle everything up. No one offered him a cup of tea.

"As I was telling Mr Watson," said the Developer, when we were all settled in the wrong places, "I was passing, so I thought I'd call in."

"Why?" said Mum.

He was a very tall man, quite thin, though Sam said afterwards that he had fat skin, and we all knew what he meant. Dad's chair was just that bit too low for him – or, at least, it might have been all right if he'd sat right back in it, but he sat on the edge so his knees stuck up, and he put his hands on his knees so his elbows stuck out sideways, and altogether he looked very uncomfortable, as if he didn't belong in a house. He'd looked much happier when he was striding about in the garden, boasting that it was all his property. His suit belonged indoors, though. It was grey and kind of shiny – not shiny because it was wearing out, but shiny because he wanted it that way.

He smiled round at all of us and he said, "I just came to

be sociable, really. Although I shan't be living in any of the new houses, I still feel I'm a new neighbour, and I wanted to call in and say 'No hard feelings?' "

"Certainly there's no need for bad feeling," said Mum briskly, "just because we disagree with everything you're doing."

The first bit of the sentence made him smile more, and the second bit made him smile less.

"Come on now, Mrs Watson," he said. "It's all over!"

It came to me that I should tap the back of my teeth with my tongue – (five times on each one of the top middle teeth, and five times where the middle teeth join, to be exact) – but also there was something I wanted to say. I'd started all this, it had been my name at the top of the petition, I didn't want Mum taking over completely. I decided to do the tapping after he'd gone. "But it isn't all over," I said, "You've put in a new Planning Application, we've had a letter about it."

It's interesting about smiles. Technically, the one he was wearing at that point was the same as the one he'd put on when he first sat down. He'd even remembered to crinkle his eyes a bit. But while the first smile had just been rather unconvincing, this one was positively unnerving.

He spread out his hands. "You must be magnanimous in victory," he said. "You do realise you've won, don't you? You've preserved that great white elephant of a house – which I shall now have to re-roof, re-wire, re-point and treat for dry rot in the cellar. My architect tells me I can turn it into three flats – whereas my original plans were for a block of ten. I've had all that taken away from me by a schoolgirl and a flock of bats, but that's the way it goes. You shouldn't be in business if you can't take reversals. I'm smiling in defeat" – he actually winked at me – "it's hardly fair of the winners to scowl at me, now is it?"

"Of course we're delighted about the house," said Mum, "but we must go along and see these new plans."

"There's no need," said the Developer. "I've complied

with all your requests. I don't think you realise how well you've done. It's extraordinary that such a tiny group of people should have made such an impact. I congratulate you."

Dad must have been thinking the same thing – that we'd done better than he'd imagined possible and that we should pat ourselves on the back and forget it – so I didn't expect him to bother to join in. But the thing was, someone was in his house who he didn't want there, interrupting routine, delaying supper, probably messing up his work schedule. So he sat forward on the sofa and he said, "We may be a tiny group of people, but you're only one person, so in fact we're in the majority. Therefore you expected to get your own way not because you've got more people on your side, but just because you've got more money."

"If you think I'm a rich man," said the Developer, "you couldn't be more wrong. Everything I have is ploughed right back into the business."

"I don't think we need to talk about money," said Mum hastily.

"I know I'm not really involved in all this," said Kathleen, swaying forward in Mum's chair and smiling at the Developer. "I'm only a visitor after all. But may I ask a question on a point that interests me very much?"

"Ask away," said the Developer. "That's why I'm here. Let's clear the air."

"Well," said Kathleen, "it seems to me that you must have bought the property without first checking whether or not Planning Permission would be granted. Wasn't that rather unwise of you?"

The Developer made a big effort to laugh, and talked through his laughing. "There wouldn't have been much point in me asking for Planning Permission if I didn't own the property, now would there?" he said, looking round at all of us as if he hoped we'd join him in laughing at such a stupid remark.

# Chapter Fifteen

But Kathleen just waited until he'd finished, and then she said, "Surely you should have made completion of the sale contingent upon Planning Permission being granted? Isn't that usual?"

There was a very short silence while the Developer tried to think of an answer and I tried to work out what Kathleen was talking about. Then I got it. Don't pay for it till you know you can do what you want with it. "*That's* why you were so cross with me that night in the garden," I said. "You were so sure you'd get permission – you didn't think you needed to wait – so you've bought it, and you've spent your money, and now you're stuck with it!"

Long before I'd finished, the Developer was holding his hand up and turning his head away, as if I was throwing things at him. He was also shaking his head slowly to and fro, as though to show that he would explain all if only I would stop throwing these imaginary things. Sam sat slumped against Dad, watching us blankly. Dad sighed and looked at his watch. Mum and Kathleen and I stared at the Developer.

"I bet you run rings round them at school," he said, when I stopped, smiling his ghastly smile. "But you're quite wrong, you know, I'm very happy with what I've bought and I'm going to make it very nice out there. Once it's finished you'll forget it was ever any different. We'll convert that house you love so much, and we'll build ten nice companions for it in its garden, and the access road will come in where the garage is now, on the far side, so it won't bother you at all – you don't love that rotting garage, do you, darling?"

I said, "Ten houses?" and at the same time Mum said, "The plans showed eight houses."

"There are a couple of extras on the new plans," said the Developer. "That's all. I have to do something to make it up to myself for losing my block of flats, don't I?"

Before we could say anything, he reached down by the

side of his chair and hitched a briefcase up onto his lap and opened it. "Now look," he said, speaking directly to me, "I know I was a bit sharp with you in the garden that first time we met, and I'm sorry about that. Even though you were trespassing, and even though you did take me by surprise, I should have been more understanding."

He took some stuff out of the briefcase. I think I was expecting him to show us the new plans, so I didn't recognise at once what it was that he was laying out on the briefcase lid. It just looked like three brightly coloured magazines. I couldn't imagine what he'd got them out for.

"I can see that you're a very sensitive person," he went on, "and I admit I wouldn't want to watch the last bits of felling and clearing myself, that sort of thing is always upsetting. So, as a gesture of goodwill, I'd like to send you – and your family of course – off on a nice little holiday for a couple of weeks, just while we clear up. A friend of mine's in the travel trade" – he handed me the magazines, which I could see were holiday brochures – "and those are the packages his company deals with. Take your pick. My card's pinned to the top one – there – with the dates when you'd do well to be away. Ring me when you've chosen where to go. Then by the time you get back, the destruction will be all over and you can settle down to watch the building."

He snapped the case shut and stood up. "I mustn't take up any more of your time," he said, to all of us in general.

We were speechless. We just watched in silence as Dad went with the Developer along the corridor to the front door, and Dad didn't say anything either, except, "Goodbye."

As soon as the front door was closed, Sam said, "Does that mean he's a nice man really? Giving us a free holiday?"

I said, "He's tried to grease my palm! That's it, isn't it? I must have *really* worried him."

Dad said, "You've already cost him money, that's what it's all about – and it looks as though he thinks you could cost him more."

Mum said, "Someone's got to get down there and see those plans tomorrow. Where's he going to put two extra houses?"

And Kathleen said, "I *am* enjoying staying here. Ron and I lead such quiet lives – it's nice to be with people who get involved with their neighbourhood."

It's always a mistake to sound too enthusiastic in our house. That was the last straw for Dad. "An Englishman's home is supposed to be his castle," he said, standing up. "Excuse me, I'm just going to the office to draw up plans for a portcullis."

# CHAPTER SIXTEEN

The holiday we didn't take had a terrific effect on us all. I'd never seen any of us – except Sam – so full of energy.

We held a mass meeting, which was more of a party really, a garden party. The guests were the five of us – most of the neighbours – one Councillor representing our MP – two reporters from the local papers, the free paper and the other one – a lawyer friend of Sarah's who could advise us on our rights – the bat-man's spirit (he'd said he couldn't come in person that night) – a chestnut tree, two poplars, three silver birches – as many birds and squirrels as were willing to stick around – and one slinky black cat which left as soon as the German Shepherd turned up.

We didn't hold it in our garden. As Dad says, there are things you can do and things you can't do, and it wouldn't have been physically possible to cram everyone in. We held it in The Garden, deciding that no one would do much about a mass trespass. Most people just climbed over or through their fences, walls or hedges. Those who really couldn't for some reason – like old Mrs Potts – came to our house and went through the missing paling in our fence.

There were very few who turned us down, though the man with the bird-splashed jeans slammed the door on us when we tried to invite him, saying he was moving anyway and that in the meantime we could tell his neighbour from him that if she chucked any more bread into her garden he was going to buy an air-gun.

At first the Councillor refused to trespass, saying we'd weaken our case if we broke the law, and she stood at the end of our garden, declaiming at people over the fence. I don't think she was even aware that in the heat of the moment she squeezed through to join us all. I think she only realised what she'd done when it was all over and she had to squeeze back again.

The Fusspots stayed firmly in their own patch throughout, standing side by side on a box and snuffling with indignation over their wall, making sure everyone knew that they heard all the various children playing in all the various gardens – not that they were complaining – and that they often heard the dog bark – not that anyone could prevent a dog barking, they knew that – and that they had been very upset by the 'brutal massacre of the orchard'. In fact most people had been a bit shocked when they saw how quickly things could be destroyed, and I suppose that's why they turned out in force.

Sam wore a badge he'd made himself which said 'Development Is An Eleven Letter Word', which he thought was incredibly witty and which none of the rest of us understood. Dad, even though it was a very warm evening, wore his chewed up grey sweater. I think he believes it protects him in some way, though I'm not sure what from.

Several people had been down to the Town Hall to see the new plans, and for those who hadn't, Kathleen had done neat little sketches so they could see what was what. The main differences – apart from the fact that the big house was to stay – was that the new houses were to be built right to the very edges of the big garden, so they'd glare right over us from a few feet away, and that the big trees were all to be felled, leaving nothing, not even the ornamental conifers.

The meeting was supposed to be informal which meant that no one did anything pompous like declaring it open, or making people take turns to speak. That sounds like a really nice idea, until it all gets going.

Sam, the two boys from the climbing frame garden, and the kids from next door to Sarah, all got together and played something mildly violent and extremely noisy up by the rockery.

Mr Dahlias made a point of plodding away from his end of things, right over to the Fusspots' fence, and saying in a loud voice that it was nice to be back in England again. Then he must have wished he hadn't bothered because the Fusspots took the opportunity to mention that when he was hammering stakes into the ground between his plants, in order to put upturned flower pots on them, the sound carried much further, they were sure, than he realised.

The bird lady fell in love with Sarah's baby and was too busy playing with it to concentrate on anything else.

The brisk, efficient lady cornered one of the Doctor MacGuires and I heard him saying, a bit desperately I thought, "I really feel you should talk to your own GP about that." The other Doctor MacGuire got into a deep discussion with one of the reporters about his planned trip to India and the 'response of the West to Hinduism.'

The other reporter was in earnest conversation with Mrs Potts, who had turned up wearing strong brown shoes, in place of her pink frondy slippers, and a watch on each wrist. I sneaked up on them, wondering what sort of interview he'd get with her, but when I got closer I could hear that he was saying, "One, two, three – it's easy to remember – dial it anytime you like and you'll get an absolutely accurate time check." And I heard Mrs Potts say firmly, "No, dear, someone else suggested that, but each time I ring it I just get a man trying to sell watches and I would never buy over the telephone."

Another group was clustered admiringly around the slinky black cat, which was arching its back to be stroked and purring, and that made me sad because Henry was still on his sick bed in hospital. Luckily I could hear Mum not far off, explaining to Sarah what had happened to him and Sarah being very sympathetic, so that helped a bit.

Anyway, the slinky black cat's flirting was cut very short when the hedge on the far side of the bird lady's garden parted suddenly. A fierce-looking man pushed through with a huge German Shepherd on the end of a chain. The little black cat slunk hurriedly over its own wall, and most of the rest of us froze, rather. I thought for a moment the Developer had set him on us – but the man explained he was just another neighbour. He worked as a night watchman, he said, with his dog, so he never answered the doorbell in daytime, on account of being asleep. But he'd heard all the commotion, he said, and had guessed what it was about, and could join us for an hour before they both had to set out to guard the derelict factory premises at the back of the High Street – which had just been bought, did we know, by our very own neighbourhood Developer? So there hadn't been much point in me suggesting they build there instead, since they were clearly going to build there as well.

The dog, he said, was as friendly as a kitten, wouldn't dream of attacking anyone unless he gave the command. That may have been true, but I noticed that no one went very close, and he didn't let it off its chain. It didn't growl or anything, but it loped about beside him very wolfishly, with its head swinging low as though it wanted us to know that its jaws were too massive for it to be able to lift it any higher without good reason. To be fair to it, though, I had stuck a leaflet half way down its throat, that time, and it hadn't bitten me. Still – even when it sat down at last, looking around from under its eyebrows and dribbling on its front foot, I decided not to go and apologise.

Sarah's lawyer friend was explaining our rights to Sarah's neighbour from the other side, but no one else was listening. The woman in the sari was telling the Fusspots she'd be very happy to write letters for anyone who didn't want to write their own, but no one else was within earshot. The Councillor was explaining to Mum and Dad that the Developer had applied to have the Preservation Orders lifted from the big trees but that if we all objected strongly enough she thought it likely that he would be told the orders had to remain, but no one else heard that.

It was the first time I'd ever understood how a teacher might feel, standing in front of a class and yelling, "I just wish you'd all concentrate."

I couldn't very well scream at them to pay attention, so I did the only thing I could think of. I began to buzz from one to the other like a midge or a wasp or something, passing everything on and then passing the comments back. Sam said afterwards that I'd looked manic, but Mum soon caught on and began to do the same thing, while Dad and Kathleen nodded admiringly from the nettlebed. "That lady over there says she'll write anyone's letters for them," I said, and, "We can save the big trees if we want to" – and, "We do have the right not to be too closely overlooked in our own homes, that man over there says so, and he's a lawyer."

I interrupted the girls next door in the middle of inviting two guys from the corner converted house to a barbecue; I interrupted a conversation about the Ganges, one about varicose veins, and one which seemed to be to do with a recipe for black pudding. Mum said later she'd destroyed the punchlines of two quite promising-sounding jokes, had stopped Mr Dahlias in the midst of an explanation about the difference between a racing pigeon and a common pigeon, and had cut in on one of the Doctor MacGuires just as he was discovering that the girl in the top flat of the converted house had a sister in Australia who lived no more than two streets away from his cousin.

The man with the German Shepherd said he'd had a very pleasant evening, and he and the dog loped off together to put the wind up intruders on the empty factory site, but everyone else stayed on until the sky got dark and the stars and bats came out. They milled about on the scorched earth where the bonfire had been, tut-tutting at the tree stumps and discussing motor-racing, the price of imported butter and the situation in the Middle East. A few bottles of wine appeared, mostly from the converted flats, the girls next door to us and the doctors, and people slid briefly back through fences and bushes to fetch glasses.

The two reporters stayed almost till last, and they must have talked about something other than India and time signals because they each said they were going to do a big story. "We'll get local public opinion on your side," said the free paper reporter, "that carries a lot of weight." "Did you know Dr MacGuire had taken some quite good photographs of the garden in its prime from the top bedroom window?" said the one from the paper you have to buy. "I'm going to use one of them to head my story." Dad said they didn't seem to be in hot competition with each other, and the free paper reporter shrugged and said, "Don't worry, we're going to use different pics."

The Councillor did stay till the very end, leaning on one of the last three apple trees, talking to Mum and Dad and me. "You've done very well," she said. "It isn't always possible to stir up as much interest as this."

"But will it do any good?" I said.

"I think so. I shall talk to the Planning Department myself, and all these people will write letters, and then the local paper stories will come out and there'll be letters from all sorts of people who didn't even know this garden existed."

"But will they really write?" I said. "They just seemed to me to be having a nice time out here." I wished we could get away from the apple trees. We already knew those last three were going to be felled, and it didn't seem quite right that they should hear us discussing how to save everything but them.

"I think they'll write," said the Councillor. "They've all heard the others say they will. No one's going to want to be the one to let everyone else down."

Dad walked Mrs Potts home. "... an electric clock," I heard him say as he led her out of our gate. "I could fix it on your wall for you."

Kathleen made tea. Sam said someone had thought his badge was very clever, but he couldn't remember who. I wrote in my diary, 'The Garden's Last Stand'.

# CHAPTER SEVENTEEN

"It's a very limited victory," I said.

"You can aim for total victory," said Kathleen, "but you don't usually get it. Don't be too scornful about compromise."

She'd given us a thick wodge of paper, made up of lots of sheets of drawing paper carefully stuck together, which had opened out into a huge family tree, very neatly typed and ruled up, a bit like the one she'd sent before she came, but with much more detail on it. Mum and Dad had said they couldn't possibly shut all that hard work away in a drawer. They suggested it should be fixed up on the slope of the attic ceiling, in memory of Kathleen's visit, and she and I were helping each other to pin it straight.

"We've lost the garden," I said, "and the crows have lost their pine."

"Yes," said Kathleen, sticking in a final tack, "but you've saved the chestnut, the poplars and two of the silver birches – the Preservation Order isn't going to be lifted on those, don't forget. He can't chop them down to build his two extra houses. And even if they 'accidentally' knock them down while they're building, they'll have to replace them – so they may as well be careful of them in the first place."

We stood back and looked at the chart. It was quite easy to read, where we'd hung it, even though it sloped away downwards. I expect we'll all get around to looking at it one of these days.

"The house was the biggest success," I said, "and the house was the thing I minded about least."

"That was before you knew about the bats. And don't forget that his ten three-storey houses have definitely been cut to eight two-storey houses. He can't build so close to you, and he can't build so high."

"True. Though if Marion Bartlett - I mean the intrepid version of Marion Bartlett – had gone on leading us, we'd probably have saved everything."

"Never!" said Kathleen. "Not from a Developer who'd already invested money. Anyway – let's be sensible about this, it was you all the time. If you hadn't done what you did, everything really would have been lost. It never really had anything to do with Marion Bartlett."

"Shame about her. I liked having an impressive ancestor."

"Family trees don't stop at the bottom line," said Kathleen. "One day you could be someone's indomitable ancestor yourself."

Good old Henry came home, purring himself into a trance when he saw us all again. The woman who'd run him over called by to enquire after him, and he even purred for her. He has a bit of a limp, which makes him look rather distinguished. He can still jump up onto the fence, but we haven't to watch while he does it because it sometimes takes two tries. Apart from that he's fine, though he keeps well away from the building works, which is wise of him.

The rest of the garden was flattened fast, the garage was smashed up and carted off, mechanical diggers made trenches, pipes were laid in the trenches, and then truckloads of breeze blocks and bricks began to arrive.

Sam doesn't spend much time on homework these days, but he is learning a lot about construction techniques.

Several of the neighbours have taken to tapping on Dad's front room office window for a chat as they pass, usually in

## Chapter Seventeen

the middle of one of his rush jobs. Someone even suggested
that as he was home all day he should be the co-ordinator of
the new Neighbourhood Watch Scheme. I've begun to be
more understanding about his paranoia. He's hung a vene-
tian blind in the window, so no one can see if he's in or out,
and he's taught the postman a secret code doorbell ring.

I do my five times tapping when I want to, but mostly I
forget, and I can never be bothered to get as far as twenty-
five. The itchy blobs are just an embarrassing memory. I'm
sure my body will come up with some other practical joke,
but at least it didn't think of anything straightaway.

Kathleen went home to Canada, but first she bought Dad
a coffee machine for his office, Mum an early morning
tea-maker, Sam a course of Karate lessons, Henry a large
freezer bag of prawns, and me a five-year-diary and a proper
briefcase, with a lock and key, to keep it private in.

There was one more thing, too. The day before Kathleen
left, a little parcel came for her, from the Midlands, with a
note saying, "We've just come across this and we thought it
might interest you." It was a small Bible, bound in brown
leather, very badly worn, especially at the corners. It was
Marion Bartlett's, of course, it had her name inside it.

"It's not a Family Bible," said Kathleen when she first
opened it, "which is a shame because Family Bibles often
have a special page or two for family information. It's just a
small travelling Bible, but it's a nice thing to have. I'm so
glad they sent it."

Then, on the morning of the day she actually did leave,
after her bags were packed and everything, she took me
aside and said, "I've got something to show you. I was
turning the pages of this last night, and look what I found."

She handed me the little old Bible, open between the Old
and the New Testaments, at the page which just said 'New
Testament' in fancy print, and nothing else. At the bottom
of that page something was written, very neatly, in Marion's
pretty writing. It said: 'We find that the parables of the

healing of the sick and of the feeding of the multitude appeal most to the trappers and Indians – the agricultural stories do not seem to catch their attention.'

"So does that mean she did go off to the wilds?" I said.

"Looks like it," said Kathleen. "Clearly there's more to be discovered about her. I'll see what I can do when I get home – I'll write to you."

"Hey!" I said. "Marion Bartlett's blood might be worth having after all, then?"

"Oh – her blood was all right for her," said Kathleen. "But I think when it comes to it your own blood's probably best for you."

# SOMETHING RARE AND SPECIAL

Judy Allen

Following her parents' divorce, Lyn has to move out of London with her mother to a temporary home on the coast. At first, missing her old friends and city life, Lyn feels like a fish out of water in this bleak, empty landscape, but then she discovers Bill Walker and his binoculars – and something very special...

This is a beautifully written and atmospheric story by the winner of the 1988 Whitbread Children's Book Award.

"A sensitive story, rich with thoughtful atmosphere."
*Junior Education*

# THE QUANTOCKS QUARTET

Ruth Elwin Harris

*The Silent Shore* (book one)
*The Beckoning Hills* (book two)

*The Quantocks Quartet* is an enthralling saga, following the fortunes of the four Purcell sisters — and their neighbours, the Mackenzie family — from the death of Mrs Purcell in 1910, through happier times (epitomized by the idyllic outing to the Quantocks) to the dark days of the Great War and its aftermath. Each book is told from a different viewpoint; the heroine of *The Silent Shore* is the youngest sister, Sarah while *The Beckoning Hills* is the story of the oldest sister, Frances.

"A winner...Vivid, solid, absorbingly interesting for its people, places, feelings...Memorable."
*The Guardian*

# THE SECRET LINE

William Corlett

Neither black nor white, Jo Carson feels ill at ease in her skin. But then Mit, a longlost childhood friend appears and takes her to the Secret Line – a mysterious section of the Underground with stations such as Heath, where she meets the engaging runaway David. But further down the line, at Jungle, danger lurks in the shape of the vicious thug Straker...

"Most interesting and most ambitious."
*The Observer*

# BAD BLOOD

### Bernard Ashley

When Ritchie's dad, Sergeant Dick Collins, is struck down by leukaemia, his best chance of survival lies in a transplant of bone marrow from a close male relative. First, though, this relative's got to be found. As this means opening old family wounds, Ritchie's quest is met by universal hostility. But is he man enough to overcome this bad blood, or will it claim him – and his dad's life – too?

"Spare and hard in content and telling."
*TES*

"Emotional suspense … Quietly thoughtful."
*The Guardian*

# GEOFFREY'S FIRST

Jon Blake

Today is the birthday of Geoffrey Stratfield Farmer – prig, snob, know-it-all and self-elected future Conservative Prime Minister. But it's also the day on which Kim McConnell – TV starlet, fledgling femme fatale and Geoffrey's classroom rival – is back at school. Which means that Geoffrey's in for some hard lessons about life in general – and sex in particular...

"A funny and moving love story... Geoffrey is an excellent creation. He is extremely funny."
*The Sunday Times*

# RUNNERS

David Skipper

It seemed like just another late summer's day to fifteen-year-old Jim Taylor when he set off for the library that morning. But when he returned a little while later with a record, in the sleeve of which young Casey had concealed data vital to the Collective's drug trafficking operation, it was the start of a terrifying and deadly nightmare. A nightmare from which he – and Casey – might never escape ...

"A well-woven tale."
*The Yorkshire Post*

"The story wallops along."
*Jan Mark, TES*

# STRAY

A. N. Wilson

Unanimously acclaimed as "a classic", A. N. Wilson's *Stray* is the wonderfully imaginative life story of an alley-cat: a tale of adventure, romance and terrible inhumanity...

"A. N. Wilson has written a classic in the sense that *Black Beauty* is a classic... His episodic, quasi-picaresque story is deeply read-on, funny, moving and exciting."
*Brigid Brophy, The Literary Review*

"A must for moggy maniacs."
*The Daily Mail*

"A cat of literary distinction, and worth meeting."
*Naomi Lewis, The Observer*

# FRANCIE AND THE BOYS

Meredith Daneman

When "quiet and vague" Francie unexpectedly gets a part in the Sir Henry Dubbs' School for Boys' play, she finds herself thrust into the limelight – and into ever closer contact with those "weird, wild alien beings commonly known as boys". Over the following months she learns a great deal about acting – its illusions and heartbreaks, as well as its glamours – and discovers that in drama, as in life, things are not always what they seem ...

"Delightful heroine ... The emotional understanding of the girl is most striking."
*Evening Standard*

"Charmingly believable ... Affectionately comic."
*The Times Educational Supplement*

# TINKER'S CAREER

## Alison Leonard

Tina was just a baby when her mother died. Now fifteen, she's determined to find out more about her. So, finding a photograph of her parents' wedding she sets out in search of her mother's family and the truth. But the truth – and with it the meaning of Tinker's Career – turns out to be even more devastating than she'd feared...

"Told at a heady pace with wonderful real, absorbing characters."
*The Guardian*

"Strong stuff."
*TES*